Rolling Stone

Adult Fiction

Rolling Stone

ISBN: 978-1-966013-01-3 Paperback

Published by Sula Too Publishing, Tampa, Florida

Printed in the United States.

Rolling Stone

By

Nadine McIlwain

Sula Too Publishing

Dedication

To my father, Willie J. Williams. It didn't matter that we never lived together under the same roof; you made a difference in my life. Thank you for always giving love and support through the joys and heartaches.

I love you, Dad.

Acknowledgments

I thank GOD and acknowledge Him in all my ways, and in all my ways, I acknowledge Him.

Thank you to the renowned and accomplished authors, Toni Morrison, Maya Angelou, and Nikki Giovanni, who set the bar high, yet attainable.

Thank you to Todd Hunter, whose professional expertise and genuine concern helped turn my dream into reality.

Thank you to my husband, William P. Massey. Without him, I would not have survived the conditions that kept me nearly bedridden for four years while I finished this novel.

Thank you to my son, Randy (Mac) McIlwain, whose skill with words provided exactly what I needed exactly when I needed it.

A special thanks to my daughter Jeaneen and her husband Jeffrey McDaniels for reviewing my manuscript and suggesting updates. They stepped in when I was about to step out.

Thank you to my grandchildren Brooklyn, who served as the model for Carmen, and J Pressley, who motivates me just by being here. God blessed me with these two.

Thank you to the members of the Still I Rise Book Club who dedicated time to convincing me I had a talent for writing, especially Erma Smith, who shares my love for reading and discussing others' stories; Jacqueline Barnes Holmes, who selflessly read my early manuscript and provided critical guidance; and Geraldine Radcliffe, who collaborated with me to edit and publish African Americans in Canton, Ohio.

Thanks to my Florida friends, Luanne Johnson Brown, PhD, Vivian Celeste Neal, Elsa Conner, and members of the Sisters in Spirit Book Club, whose engaging conversations shaped my understanding of the characters in Rolling Stone.

Thank you to Ersula Odom for pulling my book out of the ashes and relighting the spark.

Thank you to everyone in my village who helped raise me and made me believe I can.

Prologue

After their father's tragic death, five of CJ Williams' children—Franklin, Jesse, Elijah, Mirembee, and Carmen—meet for the first time. Convinced that his death was the result of a billing error by the Gas Company, the siblings decide to unite behind Mirembee to seek justice and compensation for their father's loss. Additionally, they discover that CJ's former employer used CJ's invention to make millions without compensating or acknowledging his contribution. To make matters worse, one of the siblings betrays the others, causing a rift in their mutual trust.

Their pursuit of justice involves navigating a complex network, starting with hiring Attorney Richard Stock. Stock then hires investigator Burly to locate a missing sibling. Burly not only manages to find the missing sibling but also resolves two of the Williams' main issues, leading them to seek justice for Clarence and find resolution for themselves.

"Every child grows up thinking their father is a hero or villain until they are old enough to realize that he is just a man."
— Mark Maish

Table of Contents

Book one

Chapter 1
CJ Williams

It began on the third floor, and most of the damage was limited to that area. There was very little damage on the lower level where Mirembee now stood. Water used to control the fire had soaked every inch of the lower level in dark, sooty water. Mirembee moved toward the light coming through the cracked window to see better.

Using the window light, Mirembee navigated through pools of water, tiptoeing so as not to stain the pair of black Italian leather boots Louise, who no longer wanted them, gave her. "I don't want your stupid, hand-me-down boots," Mirembee thought in her head but simply said a polite thank you to her mother. The truth was, she not only wanted them; she needed them. The brightly colored leaves on the trees and the constant honking of Canadian geese flying south forecasted an early, bitter Ohio winter. No doubt about it, she needed the boots. It wasn't that his death was unexpected. CJ Williams, Mirembee's father, was a statistic destined to live a predictable life and die younger than his white, male peers. Even actuarial data predicted a short life for CJ; smoking, heavy drinking, living in a poor, violent, crime-ridden neighborhood, and, worst of all, being single gave insurance companies the data they needed to forecast his death on their life expectancy models.

Without any knowledge of insurance companies, their actuarial data, or their death charts, as Mirembee called them, she lived in constant fear of losing her father sooner rather than later. If possible, her goal was to somehow save him, to catch him before he left this world and went to... Mirembee was not sure.

She wanted to blame her father's lack of longevity on someone or something. Louise, (her mother and CJ's use-to-be wife) was responsible, at least in part, Mirembee reasoned. Every word Louise uttered was designed to emasculate him, Mirembee thought when her mind was capable of such thoughts.

The leeches were also to blame. Mirembee called the low-lifes, hoodlums, winos, junkies, thieves, hustlers, loose women, and street whores, leeches. All of these parasites were killing her father—they drank his liquor, smoked his cigarettes, ate his food, slept in his bed (with or without him), and pissed on his floor.

At sixteen, she had accepted her parents' divorce as final and no longer prayed for their reunion. She loved her father, but spending a weekend at his house was always challenging. "Dad, how can you live like this?" She asked after witnessing LowDown unzip his pants, pull out his penis right in front of her and piss into the heating duct. LowDown's actions humiliated and embarrassed her. Humiliated at the unshielded sight of LowDown's penis and embarrassed because her father neither said nor did anything to stop this man from exposing himself, or to make her feel less ashamed for seeing him.

Mirembee knew that people called Lowdown had committed some despicable acts. 'He's a low-down dirty dog' was a label given to fathers who had impregnated their daughters or husbands who cheated on their wives and fathered outside children. Young men who attacked or assaulted senior citizens or small children were also called 'lowdowns.' She wondered what LowDown did to earn that title. CJ was non-committal about the name, but she kept asking her questions every time she saw LowDown or heard his name. She even asked LowDown himself.

"Why do they call you LowDown?" Mirembee wanted to know. LowDown looked at the young girl asking him that question. He didn't answer. Instead, he started crying and wiping his nose with the bottom of his shirt, still looking at her.

Mirembee knew her father was upset by the way he kept blinking his eyelids, tensing his facial muscles, and shifting from one foot to the other. "Why did you ask LowDown about his name?" CJ asked, nearly yelling at his daughter.

"I…I…I just wanted to know. That's all. I just wanted to know why…" Tears filled Mirembee's eyes and ran down her cheeks as she looked for something to wipe her nose.

After a long pause, CJ exploded, "LowDown had sex with his mother." It was Mirembee's weekend with her father, and this would be her memory of the weekend for the rest of her life. Reaction from her father was followed by her asking the incomplete question, "Dad…?" as she stared into her father's eyes. CJ dropped the black, cast-iron skillet he was holding into the sink and almost simultaneously lit a cigarette.

"Oh, it wasn't his fault!" CJ said emphatically, trying to smooth out his first explanation to his daughter. Although she didn't say anything, Mirembee thought, how could it not have been LowDown's fault? As if he could hear what she was thinking, CJ continued. "See, he was in prison and just got out. Had been there for almost twenty years. He didn't look like what he looked like when he went in or how he looks now. Before he got locked up, he was a good-looking man, tall, slender, and light-skinned, with the kind of hair light-skinned men and women have." CJ snubbed the butt of his cigarette into the skillet and immediately lit another. Before he released the smoke from this inhale, he studied his daughter. She had Louise in her—brazen, smart, sophisticated. Louise wouldn't need any further explanation. She would know. His daughter, her daughter, needed an explanation.

They got him. Men. Men who don't have any women around, use other men. LowDown was used many times by a whole lotta men. When he got out, he didn't know what he was. A man or a woman?

Mirembee found her voice, "So...so he RAPED his mother?" she said, slowly shaking her head from side to side in disbelief.

"Wasn't no rape!" CJ shot back. She wanted to save her son. Wanted him to know he was still a man no matter what them damn fool fagots did to him." The intensity of telling this story caused his eyes to narrow, his mouth to twitch, and his body to take on the posture of a prizefighter. He snubbed his cigarette without lighting another. LowDown needed a place to stay. He couldn't live in that house after what happened, so I let him stay here. He started drinking the day after it happened, and he never stopped." CJ's body betrayed him; his bowed head, teary eyes, and runny nose showed Mirembee that her father cared. He cared even for a man who had sex with his mother. So that's how LowDown became one of the leeches, thought Mirembee, imagining herself as LowDown's mother. She wondered what she would have done if LowDown had been her son, and I understand CJ's compassion for LowDown all at the same time.

Praised by some and criticized by others, CJ was an enigma to most but not to Mirembee, who knew her father could do better.

He was smart, street-smart, and book-smart, completing all coursework for a four-year degree, yet he never graduated. "The dean, the president, all of them goddamn educated fools changed the rules just to keep me from walking beside a white girl in the graduation processional." He told the leeches, "…I showed them. I told those motha fuckas they could keep their damn degree!" CJ embellished this story every time he told it. The version he shared with his daughter, when he thought she was old enough to understand, ended with him cussing out the college president and refusing to attend the goddamn graduation, which they had to reschedule because of the rumor CJ was planning to bomb the place.

CJ's drug of choice was alcohol. He wasn't one of those sloppy drunks who slept anywhere they could lay their heads, often pissing themselves in the process. CJ was a happy drunk, and always telling jokes followed by his own uproarious laughter.

Taking the last cigarette from his Marlboro pack and placing it between his lips, CJ let the smoke slowly escape from his nostrils and mouth at the same time. Mirembee watched him as he unscrewed the top of his favorite drink, Canadian Club Whiskey, and noticed the anticipation shining in his eyes.

She concentrated on the up and down movements of his Adam's apple as he gulped the liquor, drinking straight from the bottle still in the brown paper bag, before placing the bag and bottle back on the table.

Whiskey rushed to his brain, causing his shoulders to relax and a fleeting smile to cover his face; the smile lingered even as he nodded out. CJ struggled to keep his eyes open and to keep talking, but his speech slurred, and his eyes grew more closed than open. Alcohol and tobacco had the desired effect.

Mirembee wanted to help her father. But how could a young girl stop leeches from sucking the life out of him? How could she make Louise love him again? How could she end his drinking? What else could she do but pray? Every night, on her knees, she begged God, "Help my father… help me to help him." Each night, she received the same answer to her prayers: there is nothing you can do.

Mirembee carefully avoided visiting her father during the first five days of each month when the leeches received their government assistance checks. During those days, they would often go to CJ's one-hundred-year-old, wood-shingled three-story house which he had proudly paid eight thousand dollars for after he and Louise split up.

"This house is going to make me lots of money," he told Mirembee. "I can rent out the rooms and charge two hundred fifty dollars a month for each one. There are ten rooms in this house. That's two thousand five hundred dollars a month. I can use that kind of money to buy another rental house. Hell, I might just get me a hundred houses," he told Mirembee through glazed eyes and slurred speech.

For a while, CJ's plan seemed to work. All the rooms were rented, but Mirembee doubted if he ever consistently received much rent money. Instead, he started to accumulate belongings. Roy gave him a guitar with two missing strings in exchange for last month's rent. Skip had an old bed, which only needed the broken leg fixed. CJ could have it, and Skip promised to pay him next month. She did not want to know what Sarah Mae gave him in exchange for her rent.

"Dad, what possible use are these?" Mirembee asked as she maneuvered her way around the stack of bald tires in what should have been his living room.

"I can sell them. They're for big trucks, the eighteen-wheelers. Willie Boy didn't know how much they were worth, so I made a deal with him for two months' rent."

Mirembee didn't want to ask, but she did anyway. "Who are you going to sell them to?"

"Whoever gives me my price! Shit! I might even sell them to the city. They got trucks." CJ lit a cigarette, took a long drag, and exhaled. Through a cloud of smoke, he looked at his daughter apologetically, misreading her thoughts. "I'm sorry," he said, "I should have asked you first. Do you want to buy them?"

She observed the house filled with the leftovers of others' misfortunes. Since her father always wore what seemed to be the same long-sleeve black T-shirt and a pair of black trousers, she couldn't understand why so many shirts, ties, pants, and shoes lay in piles throughout the rooms. When he wore shoes, they always seemed to be the wrong size, either too small or too big.

Mirembee washed and ironed the clothes he wore whenever she could get him to take them off. She even tried to clean the house, at least CJ's living quarters, and organized the stuff her father refused to throw away, but nothing seemed to work. CJ's belongings appeared to multiply on their own. Week after week, whenever she visited, there was more: a broken scale, the kind usually found in a doctor's office; two more guitars, one missing its strings; a water fountain like the one in Mirembee's old elementary school, covered in rust; no fewer than twenty televisions, with and without cabinets; radios; dishes; pots; pans; glasses; tables; chairs; fans; cans of food; one dog; three cats; and thousands of roaches. Leaving his place always left a sour taste in her mouth and a queasy feeling in her stomach.

It had taken years, but finally, the Cleveland, Ohio Department of Public Health and Safety declared the house unfit for human habitation as a rental property. CJ was given thirty days to fix a list of code violations before he could rent it again. In the meantime, all tenants had to be evicted. Witnessing the leeches say goodbye to CJ, Mirembee was unexpectedly moved. In plastic bags, worn suitcases, and cardboard boxes, the leeches packed their belongings and moved out of CJ's house. It was almost ceremonial how each stopped to hug CJ before leaving. Mirembee began to understand the symbiotic relationship between her father and the leeches. They fulfilled each other's mutual needs. CJ provided the entertainment; the leeches provided the audience. LowDown was the last to leave. Even though he was stumbling drunk, LowDown seemed genuinely heartbroken that he had to leave.

"You's a good friend, CJ. You done save my life. I ain't never gonna forget you, man. And you know I'm good for that rent I owe you. I mean it, man. On the first. I be right here wit yo money."

Mirembee watched the two men embrace each other. LowDown was drunk-crying and CJ was wiping his own eyes.

Now Clarence (CJ) Williams was dead. He died in the same way he lived—an enigma, a puzzle with unconnected, scattered pieces. Even if she could connect the pieces, why should she? Some puzzles are better left unsolved, remaining forever unique and beautiful, with pieces not connected by lines. For nearly three decades of her life, sizing up the pieces and trying to find the exact fit was not Mirembee's strength. Why should it be any different now? Because CJ willed it so?

Thoughts of her father's death reignited the smoldering embers, intentionally extinguished by another fire—the loss of Mirembee's only child. That fire was different, unlike CJ's house, where you could see the damage and view the remains. Mirembee's fire burned internally, not externally. There was no visible damage. Hidden behind a shy personality, an ordinary façade, and a loveless life, the damage to her heart, mind, and thoughts was invisible.

Chapter 2

Mirembee

Tears filled Mirembee's eyes, erasing her last flicker of hope. Her father was not coming. Her mental anguish demanded to be heard, "DADDY! Please, please, please come. . . please help me!" she yelled loudly enough to grab the others' attention. In that split second, the human figures paused, frozen in obscurity. Her eyes scanned the examining room. It was not what she had expected. Everything, except the small stainless-steel sink in the corner, was white. There was too much white in this killing room, she thought. Her eyes locked on the male, who responded to her stare with, "Give 10 milligrams of Valium. I need her awake, not hysterical."

"Yes, Doctor."

Seventeen years after the U.S. Supreme Court granted the request of an unmarried, white, twenty-two-year-old woman to end her third pregnancy, Mirembee, unmarried, black, and fifteen, lay on the steel table in the back-office examination room of Dr. Donald Fitch.

Her back itched. Trying to ignore the itch, she focused on the part of her legs that was still visible. From her hip to her knee, her thighs formed a perfect V. It had only happened a few times—the V inviting her to experience the rush and calm sensations her body had come to recognize and expect. That last time led her here.

Thankfully, the white sheet, placed over the lower part of her body, covered her nakedness. Mirembee wanted to wipe the sweat from her damp, thick black hair, which threatened to return it to its natural state of curly naps and tight kinks. She wanted to scratch her back. She wanted to unclench her fists and release the side handles of that table. She wanted to, but she couldn't. A drowning man doesn't let go of his life jacket just to wipe sweat or scratch his back. Mirembee held on for life.

Had she stopped breathing? Was she already dead? If she wasn't dead, she could get up now, escape, run away, one-half of her confused mind thought. The other half hesitated. Where would you go? "DADDY! WHERE ARE YOU?" Not audible to others sharing this space, only her mind heard the scream. The female white coat pushed two pills into her mouth, allowing both halves of her mind to escape but continuing to hold her body captive.

Earlier, happier times came through the haze. Not every year, but enough times so it mattered, Cleveland Public Schools ended summer vacation and started the new school year on Mirembee's birthday. Children, herded together to get their share of the public education system, eagerly looked forward to the return, but none more than Mirembee.

Mirembee's first day of elementary school was on her sixth birthday. Daddy gave her exactly what she asked for—a brand-new tricycle with a red seat and red, white, and blue streamers flying from the handlebars. Her parents, Clarence and Louise, let her practice riding in the driveway, shared by five Black families living in different parts of a century-old house. Their house was no different from many others that had been butchered and served up to the poor residents of Cleveland, Ohio, for three hundred seventy-five dollars a month in rent; it was home for Mirembee, and she loved it.

Daddy pushed the three-wheeler from behind while Mommy waited to catch her before the wheels carried her onto deadly Glenville Avenue. Her cousins came over for Neapolitan ice cream and chocolate cake, her favorites. That night, both Mommy and Daddy listened to her prayers, tucked her in, and kissed her good night. "Rembee," they said. Louise always called her Mirembee, but Clarence called her Rembee. Tonight, they both said Rembee.

Before she would let sleep come, she insisted that they tell her once more the story of her name.

"It was your great-grandmother's name," her father began, "my grandmother. She died on the same day you were born. Lived to be 102 years old, she did."

"They said she lived so long 'cause of her name..." Louise added. "I looked it up. Mirembee means peace and long life..."

Clarence cut in, "Your great-grandmother always said, 'God

named me Mirembee 'cause He knows Ah's goin' be doin' hard times before the sun shines. Ah need a strong name if Ah gots to go through hard times before Ah get God's blessings.'

We named you Mirembee because we wanted you to be strong and to receive God's peace to see you through any hard times," Daddy said.

Sleep still hadn't come by the time she heard the man on the TV say heeeeerrrrrrre's Johnny, followed by TV laughter and the funny, breathless sounds her parents sometimes made. Tomorrow would be another good day. Smiling, she allowed sweet sleep to embrace her.

Sweet thoughts turned bitter. It was her tenth birthday, the fall of 1985. Multi-colored leaves crackled beneath small feet sporting new first-day-of-school shoes. Mirembee and her friends love matching leaf colors to crayons in their Crayola box.

"This one's magenta, and I think that one is teal."

"No! Its persimmon. Teal is like green or blue." She couldn't pinpoint the exact time or situation when the arguments began. If she remembered correctly, the arguments were always about money.

"The child needs clothes, Louise."   "Thirty dollars for one dress ain't clothes, Clarence, it's a whole damn wardrobe."

It had ruffles—the dress her daddy gave her, with yellow ruffles around the sleeves and along the hemline. Hues of reds, greens, blues, and yellows hopscotched down to her ankles over a field of purple before cascading into yellow bursts. Daddy gave her a rainbow.

"But it's Rembee's birthday, Louise," Clarence spoke in a slow, almost apologetic tone. "Please don't spoil it."

"Spoil it! I ain't tyin' ta spoil Mirembee's Birthday. I just don't know what the hell we gonna eat next week!" Louise retaliated.

"It's okay, Daddy. I don't need a new dress." Mirembee said playing the role of peacemaker, a part for which she was repeatedly cast during the past five years.

"No Rembee! The dress is yours. I worked for it, I bought it, and I paid for it. The dress is **yours**!" Clarence shouted more to Louise than to Mirembee.

Mirembee's mind linked her parents' divorce to her tenth birthday. An older, street-wiser child would have seen it coming long before, but Mirembee wasn't that kind of kid. They didn't talk; they screamed. Clarence no longer ate dinner with them. Louise no longer seemed to care. No happy, breathless sounds penetrated the paper-thin wall that divided the former master bedroom into two smaller bedrooms.

The morning following her birthday, she put on the rainbow dress and ran to her parents' bedroom to show daddy. Louise was alone.

"Where's daddy?"

"Gone."

"Where did he go? What time will…?

"He ain't comin' back. Never!" Louise said, ignoring her daughter's tears and purposefully steering her gaze away from her daughter's eyes. Mirembee had his eyes. The bond between Clarence and Louise was shattered, and not even the hallelujah prayers Mirembee learned in church could mend it. Holding back tears, Mirembee thought she hadn't even gotten a chance to say goodbye.

In the spring of her fifteenth year, she tried to cover the open wound of Clarence's departure with substitute love. An open-mouthed kiss contradicted her promise to God to never, ever let a boy do that. His hand on her breast was followed by more promises to God not to let him touch her down there. Fully clothed body rubbing followed the inevitable promise not to let him go all the way. A rubber the first time, she insisted. Promises made. Promises broken. Followed by more promises and louder prayers begging God to forgive her and to please, please, not let her be pregnant.

That summer, just before her sixteenth birthday and in the third month of her pregnancy, Mirembee tried to end her loveless life. The Clorox bleach erupted in her mouth, leaving her with a seared tongue, raw cheeks, and no taste for the cornflakes with two teaspoons of sugar in ice-cold milk, which was her pregnancy craved. She told no one about this failed attempt to defy fate. She had no one to confide in. Daddy was gone.

Remembering her father's absence helped Mirembee shake off the fog and return to the reality she lived in. She looked at the all-white room with the two figures. Was it over?

Chapter 3
CJ and Louise

Clarence James Williams, CJ to his friends, was a valued yet sometimes frustrating employee at Consolidated Electronics, Inc. It was always uncertain whether a supervisor's call would lead to praise or a scolding. Reprimands were more common, but occasionally CJ earned praise for his weekly contributions to the company's suggestion box.

Why don't you clowns put one inspector at the end of each line instead of making us carry our parts over to their tiny, air-conditioned shit-hole offices? CJ Williams asked rhetorically.

"How many times have I told you not to refer to management as clowns?" …and inspectors work in cubicles, not shithole offices." Verbal reprimands were nothing but lip-whippings to CJ. "Yes, sir," CJ told his union brothers working on the assembly line. "He sure did tongue-whip my ass," CJ bellowed, unable to contain the laughter coming straight from his belly.

CJ had the same feel for electric circuitry that Henry Ford had for the automobile assembly line and the same passion for union organizing that led Ford to fire Walter Reuther. For his knowledge of circuitry, he was valued and sought after; for his unionizing enthusiasm, he was regularly verbally criticized.

Watching CJ solve a complex set of control functions by successfully decoding and executing the logic panel was like watching a surgeon sever one vein and reattach another. As he studied the problem, he became almost trance-like in concentration. When he finished, his fingers took over, skillfully aligning one hybrid circuit with another.

It was a good job with good money, too, if you could get some overtime now and then. Maybe he and Louise would still be together if he had taken this job before they split for good. Louise was the reason he took the job in the first place, and she was the reason he left.

But that was old shit, and what his granddaddy had told him, 'If you stir up old shit, it's sho to start stinkin'. There had been enough 'stinkin' in the Clarence and Louise saga. Besides, Louise certainly did not need him now, not with the new husband.

CJ disagreed with his line buddies when they said Black people did not live like the Huxtables. The debut of The Cosby Show gave Black folks lots of beauty and barber shop talk. The Huxtables, a functional Black upper-middle-class family with traditional Black and white middle-class values, was seen as more believable than its two predecessors, Good Times and The Jeffersons. As far as CJ was concerned, JJ Evans could never have survived the projects of Cleveland's east side; he was all about shucking, jiving, and yelling

'Dyn-O-mite' every time he opened his mouth, nor could George and Louweezy Jefferson, who were also into high-class shucking and jiving. It wasn't until Bill Cosby brought the Huxtables to NBC in 1984 that CJ challenged the typical stereotypes.

The Huxtables, a Black lawyer married to a Black doctor, with smart, good-looking children all headed to college, was a far cry from the Hough neighborhood most of the assembly line workers knew.

"What you mean? Black folks don't live like that? I saw it myself. Your dumb ass ain't been nowhere … that's why you don't know nothing," CJ scolded. Some black people had succeeded. CJ knew this because he had seen his own daughter living the Huxtable life. CJ mentally stepped back from the assembly line and let his mind rewind to what had gone wrong with his family.

For the first five years after he was forced to leave his home, CJ had only seen his daughter and her mother only a few times. However, he never forgot his daughter's birthday. He would send a card or call when he couldn't face Louise in person. Louise knew he would bring a small gift for Mirembee, but she hoped he would also toss a little something her way.

Times were tough, and the small amount CJ gave often helped pay rent, buy groceries, or get a new dress or skirt.Louise told CJ about her plan to remarry on Mirembee's birthday. "It is better that you do not come to see her anymore," she said.

Following a pattern established by other Northern industrial cities, white parents moved their children out of central city neighborhoods into suburban school districts, leaving behind an area emptied of opportunities. The vacuum was filled by Black families migrating from the rural South seeking jobs and a better life in the North. Few believed their lives would be better off staying in the South and fighting the KKK and all that hate. But, instead of finding the promised land, they were welcomed to a world of underemployment, declining city services, and a police force whose job was to serve whites and protect them from the increasing number of Negroes. The only difference was, in the South, Blacks were called Neegras, but in the North, they were called Niggers.

In 1966, the smoking embers of racial unrest flared up and intensified, resulting in a fire that burned for seven days. The following year, Cleveland voters elected Carl Stokes as the first Black mayor of a major city. Sadly, his election did not trigger the revolution that those who voted for him had hoped for. By the time CJ reached adulthood, the Hough neighborhood still showed signs of the riots. Many businesses never reopened. Buildings remained boarded up, and dilapidated houses were rented at outrageous prices.

How many times had CJ driven to Shaker only to turn around without getting out of the car? Not today. His 1980 Pontiac

Bonneville showed every bit of its ten years as he entered the circular driveway in front of the gray, stone Tudor and parked behind the Mercedes with LOUISE A on the license plate. Let it be. She doesn't need me now. Go home, he told himself. Go home. Just as he started to pull away, he heard her voice.

"Daddy!" Standing in the doorway of the 'mansion' was his fourteen-year-old daughter. She looked just like her mother—curves in all the right places, smooth brown skin, and thick black hair that projected up and out away from her face, forming a perfect afro. Only her eyes revealed CJ's part in her parentage. "Daddy, Daddy. Please don't go." It had been much easier to visit before Louise remarried. But now, the gift he had for his daughter seemed too little, too late. Still, Mirembee's eyes widened as she appeared genuinely happy to see him and thankful for the lavender sweater he gave her. In CJ's mind, the sweater didn't compensate for the time he spent chasing other dreams, but it brought a smile to Mirembee's face.

"Come on in, I have something for you, too," Mirembee said while racing up the stairs. Within a minute, she bounced down the stairs, hiding something behind her back. CJ was still standing in the foyer, hoping Louise and her new husband weren't at home. Mirembee handed him a picture in a silver frame. CJ studied the picture. It confirmed his thoughts about his daughter. She had Louise's looks, an attractive, beautiful face, and a blooming body on the rise. "Remember," she said, "you gave me that dress on my tenth birthday. I wore it on picture day at school. It's the rainbow dress. Remember?" "I saved this picture for you. I knew you would like it," his child said.

CJ's eyes surveyed the rooms leading from the foyer where the two now stood, focusing on the double curved stairways and marble floors while keeping his eyes dry and his heart intact.

"Why would anyone want an all-white room?" he mumbled under his breath.

CJ wasn't just talking about the walls. The sofa, chair, tables, even the damn television were all white. White on white, he turned, taking in the full view of white furniture on a white carpet that reminded him of unspun sheep's wool. In contrast to the white living room, the dining room across the hall was dark. Two five-foot statues of Samurai warriors guarded the left and right entrances into the room, protecting the massive, vault-like furniture. Dark lacquered tops caught the sun and reflected its brightness. He turned his attention back to his daughter. He had fathered a Huxtable child living in a Huxtable world.

"Yes, I remember the dress, and you looked beautiful in it. Thank you, Baby."

"Daddy, can you stay for a while?" Mirembee asked.

"No! No! He cannot!" Louise's voice cut through the air like a paper shredder, leaving fragments of speech and thoughts torn apart. CJ saw his daughter's face void of joy.

"CJ, man, can ya let me hold five 'til payday?" The voice jolted CJ back to the present, and for that, he was grateful. CJ was thinking, and that was dangerous. The past is the past. Let it die. If he could make it to the locker room, he could get a taste from his stash, and that would help him get through the rest of the day.

"You owe me," CJ said with a grin as he took a wad of bills from his pocket and peeled off a five-dollar bill from the roll (mostly ones with the larger amounts folded on top), which always made eyes blink. CJ was generous to those who stroked his ego.

"If you turn that five into twenty, you owe me ten, man." Sometimes, they paid him back, and sometimes they didn't. When they didn't, the phone bill, electric bill, or something else wouldn't get paid that month. CJ never asked for his money. "If you a man, you pay your debts," he would always say.

His line buddies figured it out some time ago. What CJ wanted more than money was eyewitnesses to the history he was making. CJ wanted, needed his audience to serve as the connector between his dreams and his reality. As long as he could tell someone else about the ideas that crowded his mind, his dreams were real. The line was quick to oblige, with hearty appetites, they ate what CJ served and waited for the dessert.

CJ was feeling particularly good the day Louise used her court order. Although it was not unusual for CJ to be summoned to the supervisor's office, this time, the summons came from the plant manager. Something serious was happening. CJ expected more than the usual lip-whipping or hand-spanking as he approached the air-conditioned office on the other side of the plant.

"You're Clarence Williams," the manager began.

"Yessss!" CJ responded apprehensively while still standing.

"You have been with the company for … let's see," the manager said, looking through the manila folder on his desk, "for four years. Correct?"

Now CJ was getting nervous. Even though this job was just like the assembly line, all the time moving but going nowhere, CJ did not want to get fired. Clarence James Williams fires companies, they don't fire him. He replied with a self-assurance that bordered on cockiness. "Yes, that is correct."

"And you... let's see, you've been dropping an idea in the suggestion box every week since you've been here?" Whatever he wanted, CJ was hoping he'd get to the point. This time, CJ didn't respond. "Well, let me be the first to congratulate you. The top brass liked your idea for packaging the adapters," he continued. CJ felt some tension leave his shoulders and decided on his own that he would sit down, since the asshole never invited him to do so. He listened as the plant manager explained how they were able to speed up the production line using CJ's suggestion. He finished with a promise to CJ to expect a nice bonus in his next paycheck. CJ left the manager's office, greeted by a chorus of congratulations from everyone except his Mr. I-got-a-damn-engineering-degree-but-don't-know-shit supervisor.

As CJ exaggerated the events that took place in the plant manager's office, the police arrived, handcuffed CJ, and escorted him out of the factory. Rumors spread that the mighty CJ was arrested for non-support and was living off the county. In reality, it wasn't confinement in the Cuyahoga County Correctional Center that kept CJ from returning to work. Instead, he was held back by two of the seven deadly sins and their close cousin. Vanity wouldn't let him bow his head before those he didn't respect. Humiliation stopped him from facing the knowing stares of the line. Pride kept him from even considering walking back into that factory, even if it meant losing his last paycheck. CJ was released after spending three days in Pissville and walked home to find the letter Mirembee had written five days earlier.

Dear Daddy,

I wanted to tell you when you came by last week, but Louise wouldn't let me. I'm pregnant, Daddy. I'm sorry, but I am pregnant. Mom wants me to get rid of it, but I don't want to. Help me, please. Can I live with you, please? You have to come and get me today. She is making me go to the doctor tomorrow. If I have an abortion, will I go to hell? Please help me Daddy. I love you. Please, please, please come.

I love you,

Your daughter,

Rembee

Handcuffs bound both his hands and his spirit. What could he do to help his beloved daughter? He lost his job and didn't have enough cash to pay his bills by the first of the month, let alone provide for himself and Rembee. He was a broken man—no money, no job—living in one room of a boarding house now infested with rats and crawling cockroaches. There was no way he could give his daughter a life in Shaker Heights. His pockets were empty. It was too late. Louise had succeeded where many others had failed. She had broken him.

Chapter 4

Louise and CJ

Many tried to break his spirit, starting with his schoolteachers and later the men who supervised his employment. The women, including the mothers of his children, vexed him the most. As soon as they got pregnant, they began pressuring him to get married, punch a time clock, and buy a house. Only Louise, Mirembee's mother, managed to get him to share her bed under the legal permission of the state of Ohio.

At first, his admiration for Louise replaced love. She was strong, smart, and independent, just like him. Men envied him when he was with Louise. She wasn't Lena Horne beautiful, but she was Eartha Kitt built. Lord, was she built. An athlete's body, muscular in all the right places, housed her quick mind. Legs made for running were accentuated by tight skirts and high heels. CJ often said that V-neck sweaters were invented so Louise's rounded breasts could give men something to dream about at night.

Her long neck supported a head topped with thick, dark hair styled in an upsweep that added to her height. Big brown eyes with long lashes attracted many men before they were sidetracked by her wide nose and thick, protruding lips. Her smile often brought them back if her body hadn't already done the trick. Louise flashed white, even teeth—the envy of white girls whose parents spent small fortunes on orthodontists. This time, CJ proposed marriage, on the day his daughter was born.

Mirembee was Louise's clone except for her gray-green eyes that mirrored her father's and her skin color. Where Louise was ebony, Rembee was mahogany, a blend of Louise's dark skin and CJ's lighter tone. They agreed on the name Mirembee for their baby girl, but CJ called her Rembee. He adored his daughter, and she loved him. But, exchanging marriage vows, which was supposed to bring them closer, seemed to push them apart. Within weeks of their marriage, Louise started to work on him. "Jean said Billy got on at the Ford plant. He's making ten dollars an hour."

"Don't start that again!"

"But Clarence, we'll never have nothin' but this old. . ," her hand waved the air of the former parlor turned four-room apartment. "Why can't you just get a regular job?"

"Louise, baby, come look at this! It's gonna make us millionaires." CJ knew that the lines and circles connecting at odd points on a piece of paper meant little to Louise, but he wanted her support. Her look spoke louder than her voice. Billy's new job was Jean's ticket out of this squalor. CJ's paper meant more of the same old shit.... scraping to make ends meet.

"Look, baby," Louise said using the same sexy charm that had gotten to CJ in the first place, "I know one day you gonna make it. But…"

CJ interrupted the familiar and unwelcome refrain, "All right, damn it! I'll go down to that goddam Ford plant tomorrow!"

"You promise?" Louise said, the disbelief evident in the inflection of her voice.

"Yeah, yeah. I'll go tomorrow."

"I love you, Clarence."

Previous discussions ending like this culminated in some serious fucking. But not this time. Louise was saving herself until after Clarence got the job. CJ, on the other hand, was not saving himself and was sure he could find a warm, moist teacake tonight, tomorrow, or anytime he wanted. If Louise was not willing, many other females were.

CJ was immediately hired at the Ford plant after scoring 100 percent on the lack of intelligence test, as CJ called it, and charming, almost charming the pants off, the personnel assistance who administered it.

Louise was elated. Her elation led her to spend the money as fast as CJ could make it. His generosity with his paycheck was matched by Louise's generosity in bed. Louise was happy. CJ was stifled. Ten months later, CJ announced that he had quit that fuckin job.

"You what?" shouted Louise.

"Look baby, those assholes at that plant ain't about shit. I know more about production than they'll ever know. Besides, they used my goddam idea and up the line production twenty-five percent. Mothafuckers didn't even acknowledge it was my idea. Fuckin' supervisor took credit for the whole goddam thing."

Raging anger gripped both the man and the woman. "You didn't have to quit! What are we going to do now?" Louise's voice raised an octave with each word.

"I'll work it out. Trust me Baby. I'm on the verge. As soon as I work out a few bugs, I'll be ready to sell the circuit adapter. Baby, it'll be worth millions. Trust me."

"Trust you!" The anger and rage in her voice made the words sound like epitaphs. "Trust you, what the hell you think I been doing for the past year… the past ten years, Clarence!"

This time, Clarence said, "I've had it. I can't do this anymore."

"Look, baby, I'll get another job. You know me. I can get a job." It was true CJ could get a job; he just couldn't keep one.

"Clarence, we have a child. She needs things. I need things." As though 'to be continued was written across her forehead, Louise turned to leave the bedroom. CJ blocked her exit.

"What you want that ole CJ can't git you, baby?" He spoke slowly as he moved closer to her. "What you need that CJ don't have?" His lips gently touched her cheek despite her protests. "Tell CJ what you need, Baby." Hot breath warmed her body as he exhaled into her ear. Heightened senses fueled Louise's involuntary moan as his hand explored her body. CJ gave up trying to control Louise's mind, but her body responded like bees to honey whenever he met her lips.

There was something about CJ she couldn't, wouldn't deny herself. She parted her lips, took in his tongue, and felt herself getting moist below.

They barely made it to the bed before he removed her panties slowly and deliberately. She watched while he took them, laid them open to the crotch and inhaled her scent. Louise's body raged. His mouth went to her breasts. Left then right. She arched her back. His hand explored the extent of her body, gently passing over the mound of pubic hair, hesitating for a moment at the opening below, leaving an impression that begged its return.

"Now," she whispered hoarsely.

"No, not yet." He removed the rest of her clothing. CJ seems to time and react to her sexual intervals just as an expectant husband aids his pregnant wife during pre-birth contractions. Almost there, honey. Keep breathing. He assisted her progression with caresses to her body. Hold on, honey, almost time. His head lowered and sought that spot between her legs, which women use as leverage, and men are known to kill for. Lips and tongue moved her to a plateau that rendered her breathless and light-headed. Louise's mind and body were together now, anticipating the imminent explosion. He took her very gently. How long they remained one body, Louise neither knew nor cared. Together, lost inside carnal pleasure, mutual climax came, more like the slow eruption of a long-dormant volcano than the explosion of a bomb.

CJ remained unemployed for the next six months, and Louise had to reapply for welfare.

A chance encounter with Louise's old friend, Jean, changed their lives. Jean was always beautiful, and her recent makeover accentuated her stunning looks. Clarence watched Louise's eyes as they scanned Jean's appearance, from her freshly dyed auburn hair to her elegant gray suit paired with matching leather shoes, gloves, and bag. He could tell that Louise was only half-paying attention as Jean, with clear self-satisfaction, shared updates about Billy's job promotions and their new house. Clarence could only imagine what was going through Louise's mind. Louise had gained some weight.

Six months after that encounter, the day after Mirembee's tenth birthday, Louise told Clarence to get a steady job or get out. This time CJ knew she was serious. Observable changes had occurred in Louise. Losing weight and exercising had restored her physical beauty. Having an affair restored her self-confidence. CJ left Louise and Mirembee that day.

Chapter 5

CJ, Amy and Jesse

Amy Proctor was the country girl Johnny Lee sang about, looking for love in all the wrong places. She was the kindest, gentlest woman God ever put on this earth. Amy couldn't say no to anyone. As a result, Jesse Williams Proctor was the illegitimate son of Clarence (CJ) Williams and the fourth of Amy's six multi-colored children, all of whom her mother adored.

It was Amy's duty, as she saw it, to ensure that each of her children knew their fathers by sight, if they still came around, or by name if only their imprint on the faces of her children remained. Amy gave each child their father's last name as a middle name, even if their daddies refused to acknowledge paternity. Amy's view of the relationships that spawned her children was always remembered and told to her children through proverbial rose-colored glasses. No mention was ever made of the mornings when she would awake alone, feeling like one of those rags she used to clean toilets.

CJ was the only one who was already married, a fact for which Amy was in a constant state of apology. "If I'd known that CJ was married, I wouldn't have had nothing to do with him. Nothing! Never!" Amy told Jesse. Amy believed it was important to raise her children with proper morals. And as far as Amy knew, there was only one moral law: do unto others as you would have them do unto you. "I wouldn't want no woman messing with my husband," husbandless Amy said.

Amy met CJ at Wilson's Electrical Supply, where they both worked. He, a temporary worker, managed inventory, while she, a lavatory attendant, cleaned the toilets. When he told her that she smelled good, Amy knew it wasn't, couldn't be true, but she cherished hearing those words from CJ. All 120 pounds of this small, frail woman, who cut her own brown hair—short in the back and long enough on the front and sides to shield her face—wanted to believe him. Any woman with three illegitimate kids, living in apartment 13D of the Revere Estates on Cleveland's West Side, would be happy that this big, handsome man with the strange eyes even noticed her, let alone paid her a compliment.

"Hey, little lady, what's your name?" CJ grinned at Amy as she came out of the lavatory, bucket in hand, scarf wrapped around her head, the pungent smell of Lysol wafting from her skin. "You sure smell goooood."

She knew his name. He was CJ Williams. Always talking loudly, saying things to everyone, giving people money, and now telling her, 'SHE smelled good.' She wanted to believe him. Every rhythmic beat in her heart wanted to believe him. "What you wanna know for?" she asked, her hair showing parts of her face but hiding her downcast eyes, a favored pose.

"I always want to know the names of pretty little ladies who smell so fresh and clean," CJ offered.

Amy responded, hearing "fresh and clean" as though he said "young and beautiful," "Mah name's Amy. Amy Proctor, and I know who you are, Mr. CJ Williams," she announced.

"The name's Clarence James Williams. And now I know your name," CJ said, smiling and entering the lavatory.

During the next week, Amy tried to time her cleaning with CJ's breaks, but timing and good luck were as foreign to Amy as compassion was to members of the Ku Klux Klan. Forget about Mr. Clarence James Williams and those eyes of his, she told herself.

"Give you a ride home, pretty lady?" CJ asked, catching her completely off guard. Without waiting for an answer, CJ slid his arm under hers and helped her into the passenger seat of his car. The ride home took them from the near-deserted east side industrial area through the flats along Lake Erie to the near west side. Amy said nothing; she didn't have to. CJ never stopped talking.

"I got big plans. Someday I'm gonna make lots of money. You see, I got me this circuit adapter. You know what a circuit adapter is, don't you, little lady?"

It seemed to Amy that CJ didn't really want an answer, since he never stopped talking long enough for anyone to answer, let alone someone like Amy. If those teenage boys hadn't been hanging out under the streetlight in front of her apartment, Amy would have just let CJ continue talking and drive away. They were the same teenage boys always cussing and calling her children 'goddam half-breeds, Sambos, and Pablos.'

"Niggers and nigger-lovers should stay on the east side!" they yelled. While Amy could live with the name-calling directed at her, her heart broke when the boys called her children those names.

Seeing those boys, Amy interrupted CJ's incessant talking, "Them boys ain't no good. Always talkin bout people." CJ, startled by the tiny voice, stopped talking.

"They've been talking about you?" he asked. Amy did not want any trouble, so she hesitated to answer.

"No," she said unenthusiastically, not even convincing herself. The car stopped. CJ opened his door, and before Amy could find the handle to open her door, it swung open, and CJ extended his hand to Amy. She accepted and placed her arm around his as they walked to her door.

Amy tensed as CJ stopped and walked toward the boys whose eyes were fixed on the Black man and white woman walking arm in arm. "Wait here," he said.

CJ didn't want Amy to hear him, so he spoke just loud enough for the boys to hear. "Which one of you wants to be a woman?" CJ said as he approached the one with the biggest head and smallest balls.

"Nig…"

The streetlight above drew four sets of eyes to the object reflecting in CJ's hand, like a spotlight highlighting a monologue on stage. If this scene were staged, CJ was now the star. "Seems like if you want to fight women, then just to make it fair, you ought to be one. So, which one of you wants to be a woman?"

Another opened mouth fell silent as the razor drew its first blood. Surprised by the blood but more embarrassed by the warmth trickling down his pant leg, the youngest slowly backed away. Muscles of a boy are no match for muscles of a man. With little effort, CJ simply picked up the boy and threw him. CJ grabbed the closest one to him, flipped him to the ground, and whispered, "You the one? You tired of being a boy? You want to be a woman?"

Razor raised; CJ's hand came down quickly. Too quick for even young eyes to see, too quick for a young body to feel pain. Not too quick for the mind to imagine death. Point made; CJ watched as the other three began to run before he turned his attention back to the remaining boy. Had this clown fainted, CJ wondered? He shook the boy to wake him but left him lying there. This time, CJ wanted Amy to hear him. "And I will be back if any of you bother this lady again."

Amy stood frozen, witnessing this scene. She thought she saw CJ pull something from his pocket that momentarily caught the reflection of the streetlight. She wanted to yell at those boys as they began to circle CJ, but her mouth went dry. Before she could speak or move, CJ somehow lifted the tall one and threw him about three feet in the opposite direction. CJ had the loud-mouthed one down on the ground. 'Don't kill him,' Amy mouthed silently. The other two were running in the opposite direction when CJ released the third boy. Amy only heard CJ say, "And I will be back, if any of you motherfuckers bother this lady again."

That ride home ended with CJ in Amy's bed. His caresses restored some of her dignity that other men had shit on. Amy had no idea that a fight with Louise led CJ to warm her bed that night. She didn't realize that Louise's nagging had driven CJ to take this menial labor job in the first place. All Amy knew or cared about was that strong, handsome CJ had made love to her that night, not fucked her. Of all the women in the factory, of all the women in the world, he had chosen her, kissed her, caressed her, touched her—and most importantly, CJ Williams defended her and her children against those hoodlums outside.

Amy's mind struggled to understand the details of CJ's plans and the complexity of the circuitry he showed her. He tried to explain things simply, but her thinking was more focused on repetitive manual work, while he used the vivid and elaborate language of technology.

Over the following months, CJ continued driving Amy home, and if the menacing boys were lurking nearby, he would stay the night. Amy found herself wishing, even praying, that each evening CJ's car headlights would reveal two or three of those tough-looking, leather-clad, tattooed boys. After their initial encounter, Amy half-expected them to retaliate somehow—perhaps by pelting her door with eggs or vandalizing her apartment building's walls like they had the year before. She also thought they might damage CJ's car. But they didn't. The boys, who had been so confrontational with her and her children, decided to leave them alone after their one encounter with Amy's protector.

Amy lay fulfilled in CJ's arms. Her admiration for him was mutual about twice a month. Although she had known other men who she thought loved her, they never treated her the way CJ did. CJ talked to her about important things like his inventions and electrical stuff. And it didn't matter that he wasn't white. For Amy, her thoughts were unthinkable. Does this man love me? Does he really, really love ME? Would he even consider marrying…?

"CJ?"

"Yes, sweet pea?"

"I know I am not as smart as you…"

"Wait just a minute," CJ stopped her. "Why you always putting yourself down? Didn't I tell you to hold your head high and your ass higher?" CJ chuckled.

"I know, I know. But…" Amy decided to be uncharacteristically bold. "I want to marry you, CJ. I love you more than any man I've ever known. I know I have those three children, but they love you, and I know you must love them because you're always doing things for us. I can be a good wife for you. You can move in with us, or we can live with you in your house, and you won't have to do anything except what you've been doing, and…" Amy realized she had been talking nonstop, and CJ hadn't interrupted her. This unusual silence from a man who was always talking left Amy feeling puzzled.

"CJ…?" she finally asked.

"Sweet Pea, I... I... I am married. I thought you knew. I have a wife. I can't have no two wives."

A wave of nausea hit Amy. The orange juice she drank for breakfast threatened to come back up. "God, please don't let me throw up now," she silently prayed. "CJ, I'm pregnant," Amy confessed. At that moment, Amy fully expected CJ to get up, put on his clothes, and walk out the door, just as the others had. The fact that he stayed by her side confused Amy.

Not knowing what to say, he waited before speaking. "I've got children, three, maybe four of them. I'm their father. And if this one is the fifth, I'm going to be its father, too," he said, gently rubbing her belly. "I should've known this was going to happen. I guess I did know," Amy listened as CJ's voice grew softer. She snuggled closer, wrapped in the cocoon of his large body. "Our child will grow up knowing that Clarence James Williams is its father," CJ assured her. "But I cannot marry you."

Out of their mutual need for each other, Jesse was born, two years after Rembee. Jesse was exceptionally handsome. He inherited a keen nose, a sharp chin, thick eyebrows, and Ricky Ricardo-like hair from the combination of his black father and white mother. His greenish-gray eyes and full lips were traits from CJ's side. The golden bronze skin was a blend of their heritage, giving him a perpetually suntanned appearance.

Jesse inherited physical and mental traits from both of his parents. He had quick hands but a slow mind. While he could follow instructions and complete tasks when shown, his deductive reasoning skills were limited. It was clear early on that Jesse's role in life would often be that of a follower.

His father, who visited him but never took him anywhere, fascinated Jesse. He didn't know where his father lived or worked, but he knew that his father could fix things. With little effort, CJ was able to restore sound to a broken radio or make a non-working TV produce a clear picture and sound. Jesse watched CJ rewire an old lamp and even craft a shade from old curtains and wire. When Amy's paycheck fell short, CJ cleverly connected to a neighbor's electricity. To Jesse, CJ was the smartest man he had ever met, and he wanted to be just like his father. Every repair CJ made was followed by Jesse's curious questions.

Why did you connect the black and red wires to each other?

How much glue do you need?

What happens if I disconnect this cord?

Is this the right size battery?

How do you know when it reaches the right temperature?

CJ, with the patience of a kindergarten teacher, took the time to carefully answer all of Jesse's questions. At first, he provided brief explanations, but as he realized Jesse's limited understanding, CJ began using diagrams, charts, and even stick figures to help clarify his points. Both of them were overjoyed when Jesse demonstrated his comprehension. Father and son worked together, and CJ saw that while Jesse might be slow to think, he was quick with his hands. For CJ, this meant offering extra care and providing as much guidance as possible to his son. "A man who uses his hands for work and not his mind has to work extra hard," CJ told Jesse. "He needs to be better than the best."

Jesse eagerly looked forward to the days when his father would visit the house, bringing gifts for the whole family, including his mother, sister, and brothers.

When Jesse was eight years old, CJ introduced him to his sister, Rembee. This introduction consisted of a series of snapshots. CJ told his son, "Jesse, this is your sister, Rembee. Someday, the three of us will leave this old place, boy. When I finish this project, I'm going to buy the biggest house you've ever seen. You, me, and Rembee will live together and say to hell with this whole world." The snapshots showed Rembee at three months old, six months old, her first steps, her first birthday, and even her trip to the zoo.

Jesse asked, "CJ, why can't you and Rembee come live with Mama and us now?"

CJ replied, "We just can't, son. That's all! But someday soon, all of us will live together and have a great life. That's why I want you to know your sister."

"Does she know me?" Jesse asked, even though he knew the answer. He understood that CJ never showed Rembee any pictures of him. In his short life, he couldn't remember CJ or his mother ever taking pictures of him.

"No, son," CJ said, "her mother ain't like yours."

Chapter 6

Mirembee's Abortion

The room was cold, and Mirembee shivered on the examination table, her feet in the stirrups. She wondered how long it would take as she looked around, waiting for the doctor and his nurse to finish their preparations.

She mused to herself, "So, this is the room where they kill babies." Everything was white, milky white and clean. "Thou shalt not seethe a kid in its mother's milk," Mirembee recalled Janet, her best friend since moving to Shaker, explaining why she couldn't eat the cheeseburger Mirembee offered.

"We believe the milk of the mother is given by God to nourish the young and should not be associated with their death," Janet had explained. *What would Jewish Janet think about this milky white killing room? Today, no young would be nourished here,* Mirembee thought.

"If I were a speck on the wall, she would wipe me off. If I were her new car, she would have me washed weekly. Maybe if I were her husband, at least she would yell at me. But I am only her daughter. She doesn't even notice me." Mirembee's admission brought tears to Janet's eyes.

The room felt smaller than when Louise first forced her to come here. Mirembee had managed to hide her pregnancy for three months. In fact, Mirembee thought she could have had the baby right in front of Louise's face, and she wouldn't have noticed.

"You're going to have an abortion!" Louise spat these words at her only daughter. Too stunned to object and too beaten to protest, Mirembee simply gave up and allowed Louise to dominate. "There is no way I am going to be a grandmother, not now." Within the week, 'It must be done right away,' the doctor said, and Mirembee waited for the inevitable.

Eye-level with Mirembee as she lay on the examining table with her feet in the cold stirrups, there was a sink on the right. On the left side of the room, there was a desk and a small stool for the doctor to sit on, she guessed. The desk contained many pamphlets and, believe it or not, some blank prescription pads. Boy, Mirembee smiled, I know some heads who would really like to have those. The brochures, from what Mirembee could see, were all about babies. BIRTH CONTROL, NURSING, THE JOY OF BEING PREGNANT, MOTHERHOOD AND YOUR FIRST BABY.

How could she do this to me? Mirembee closed her eyes, hoping to shut out the reality of the moment. The only person she had ever let see her naked was her child's daddy, and now this perfect stranger and his nurse were looking at, probing, touching, and discussing her as though she wasn't even there.

On the first visit, this doctor, the cheapest and least known one Louise could find, without warning, made a fist and pressed it to Mirembee's vaginal opening. The gesture was so unexpected that all she could think about was the moisture on her panties. The milky discharge, her constant companion since she let him do it without the rubber, flowed from her body through her panties to this doctor's fist. The embarrassment and humiliation that engulfed her appeared to go unnoticed by her mother. She heard Louise explain to the doctor that her daughter was here for an abortion, and he didn't need to measure.

Two days prior to this final visit, they had inserted the laminaria to dilate her cervix. Mirembee cried the entire time. Louise asked questions. Mirembee knew she wasn't the first girl to get pregnant or to have an abortion, but Mirembee had felt her baby... move. Today, she would have the abortion.

For a moment, the external tears dried, and her mouth contained no spit. She was mentally getting off the examining table and putting on her clothes. Her father had come and put an end to this nonsense. CJ was here to save her. The shock of the cold steel speculum invaded her vaginal canal, ripping the thoughts out of her head like a lightning strike illuminates a darkened sky.

Drowsy from the Valium, Mirembee could barely make out the doctor's words.

"Mirembee! Do you understand what we are going to do?"

"Yes." That's not my voice. I do not understand why they want to kill my baby. "It'll be all right, doctor," the voice said. "Let's just get it over with so we can get outta here."

"Please, Mrs. Williams, it is less traumatic for these girls if they know what to expect."

Mrs. Williams. Louise. Mother. It's her mother's voice. Reality tried to penetrate the haze.

"I've already told her everything she needs to know," Louise responded to the doctor's statement. The look on the nurse's face conveyed thoughts that would surely lead to her dismissal if they had been spoken aloud.

Mrs. Williams, you're here because your daughter is very young and could use your support. If you won't let me follow procedure, I will have to insist that you leave the room.

"Ascot. My name is Mrs. Ascot." Then, the voice was silenced.

Now, Mirembee, you will feel pressure to go to the bathroom, but you won't have to urinate... you won't have to pee. We will control the pressure. Understand?

Mirembee said, "Yes." Did daddy get my letter? Stop them, daddy! Please, don't let them...

"Open your legs, Mirembee. Wider. That's it. Relax. Open! Open wider! Okay, nurse, we're ready for the epidural."

Louise, I know you are here. Please stop them. Don't let these strangers touch me. I promise I'll be good. I won't let him do it again. I promise I will clean the house. I will do whatever you want me to... please. Silent pleas fell on deaf ears.

"The instrument is a little cold, Mirembee. After a second or two, it'll warm."

"Okay."

"It doesn't hurt, does it?"

"No." She felt nothing. It was as if her lower body was part of another time, unconnected to her presence.

"You may feel a slight pulling in your stomach. It's okay. Just let go when you feel the pressure being released. Nurse, forceps?"

"Here you are, doctor."

Mirembee's mind played the entire scene in slow motion. Minutes lasted hours as a slow, steady stream of hot fire trickled from her.

The mirror that enabled happy mothers to see their child's birth had not been turned. Mirembee watched as the male white coat used forceps to pull the baby's legs from her. A girl, I will call her Fortunate. Mirembee saw the tiny feet with tiny toes, each separated from the other just like CJ's. The baby's body looked ghostly white, as though covered with a shroud. *It's okay. That's just the birth sac, she thought, recalling a lesson from health class. It was so tiny, Mirembee could hardly believe the little hands were grabbing and releasing, and the feet were kicking.* Mirembee wanted to see the baby's face and head. *Would she have hair? No matter what anyone said, little bald babies were not cute. The head,* thought Mirembee, and she gave another involuntary mental push. Something was wrong. Like one of those dreams where you run as hard and as fast as you can, but with each step, your destination gets further and further away. The white coat was holding her baby's head inside Mirembee's body. Mirembee screamed in her head as loud as she could. I want to see her face.

"Catheter. Now!"

"Yes, doctor."

Mirembee heard a suction sound, like a vacuum cleaner. Louise was always cleaning. Why now? Mirembee's muddled mind wondered. She watched as her daughter's little arms jerked out in an involuntary quick spasm like someone surprised by an electric shock. Mirembee watched as her baby's fingers and toes separated as though they had touched a too-hot handle. Mirembee continued to stare as the little fingers and toes slowly came back together… limp, lifeless little. . . the head…hair.

The white coat removed what was her summer of passion, her one time when she had not let him spill his seed, her child, her baby. A plastic bag. No! Not a plastic bag.

Mirembee heard singing—soft, plaintive singing, a single voice with no accompaniment—low, clear, and mournful. It was the kind of song movie directors use when they want the audience to leave their current place and slip onto the screen with the actors. Mirembee was acting in a dramatic scene that would end as soon as the word 'cut' was spoken.

"There, Mirembee, it's all over. You are no longer pregnant."

"When can we get out of here?"

"As soon as we clean her up, Mrs. Wil … Mrs. Ascot. In about an hour."

Time didn't matter to Mirembee; she surveyed the room again, no longer the color of life-giving milk. Now all she saw was red, the color of blood, the color of death.

Mirembee, it's time to go. Put your skirt on." They left the clinic ninety minutes after arriving. It was lunchtime. Louise was dressed elegantly in a crisp white linen suit with solid black buttons on a double-breasted jacket. A white turban hat sat atop her head, allowing her long black hair to bounce freely. Her black leather Coach bag, bought secondhand, made her appear more affluent than she actually was. She had married well the second time around, but her lean years taught her restraint. Money was saved for the inevitable rainy day. Not even her current husband, Lee Ascot, knew the extent of her assets in her private, separate account.

As they walked through the parking lot, several men's eyes focused on Louise. While she opened the car door for Mirembee and got into the driver's seat, men's approvingly sexual glances followed her.

"Are you hungry, Mirembee? We can stop for a sandwich and a shake at the burger place," Louise tried to sound upbeat. "How about that one around the corner?" Mirembee knew Louise hated fast food, and the empty gesture was meant to appease the wrong Louise had done.

"No," Mirembee sighed, "It's wrong to seethe a kid in its mother's milk." Louise gave her a quizzical glance. "From now on, I want you to call me Rembee!"

Mother and daughter drove the rest of the way home in silence. Rembee made a mental vow to herself. Never again would she allow anyone to take away something that was hers, something she loved. From now on, she would be her father's child: strong, confident, independent of any man or woman, and, most importantly, unafraid of anyone.

Chapter 7

CJ and Evelyn

Two weeks after Evelyn's birthday passed without much notice, the blood came, followed by her grandmother's command to, "tear a piece off of dis here sheet, wrap it 'round dis here paper and stick it 'tween your legs," followed by her warning to "stay 'way from dem boys." That was the extent of sex education for poor black girls like Evelyn, coming of age as Eisenhower's recession claimed its first victims. It was the same lesson that Evelyn's mother received from the same source.

Evelyn and her mother had a simple, non-relationship. The two barely spoke to each other and both followed Evelyn's mother's instructions. For church, Evelyn had to wear what she called "old ladies' clothes." The long dresses were bad enough, but she was also forced to wear a hat; she was the only girl in the entire church under 30 who had to keep a hat on her head.

Suspicion was the main emotion shared between Evelyn and her grandmother. Evelyn watched Gram watch her. It seemed that no matter where Evelyn went, she could feel Gram's presence. She had to find out, thought Evelyn.

Long before this happened, she had to know. Even at sixteen, Evelyn was a good mother. She raised Franklin with a touch of intelligence and a bucket full of mother wit. Now, she was about to become a grandmother before her thirtieth birthday, and her son refused to accept any responsibility for the child he helped to create. Thinking about her soon-to-be-born grandchild brought back old memories, laid to rest but never entombed.

Neighborhood bullies mocked her matted hair and torn clothes until CJ told them to shut the hell up and leave her the hell alone.

"Thank you," a shy, unattractive Evelyn said to CJ after one particularly cruel taunting by those boys.

"Well, well," said CJ, "she does talk."

Evelyn watched as CJ quickly raised his hand and pinched his nostrils shut with his thumb and index finger. To hide the gesture, CJ rubbed his upper lip and quickly lowered his hand to his side. The quick action and his attempt to cover it up didn't escape Evelyn's notice. Even if CJ helped her this time, he was no different from the others.

"Sho", I can talk. I can talk just like you and dem other heathens!" she spat.

"Hold on now. I'm not the enemy," he said, smiling and seeming to adjust his nose a little. "My name's Clarence, but people just call me CJ."

"I knows who you is!" she said and quickly added, "…and I don't care!" She lied. The 1960s were tough times for girls like Evelyn. She lived in shadows, watching the world from dark corners and praying for the sunlight that never shone on her face. She knew she wasn't pretty and believed she was ugly. Her grandmother made sure of that, publicly degrading Evelyn about her too-big lips, squinty eyes, dark skin, short nappy hair, and skinny body with dangling arms and legs. Evelyn accepted the fact that she smelled badly, although she could never smell anything, since the other kids called her 'stinkweed' and held their noses when she came around. Evelyn's other senses confirmed she was a child of unfulfilled needs, trying to satisfy her needs and wants with prayer and an imaginary life.

Like refugees fleeing war-torn countries only to find conditions as bad or worse in their new sanctuary, Evelyn let her imagination take over where reality failed her. From her corners, she watched the white girls, and their boyfriends walk hand-in-hand to the movies. Outwardly, she acted as if she didn't notice, but inside, she wished she could be just like them, praying, "Give me long, wavy hair like Marilyn, please God, make my skin white like Jennifer, and please, God, give me a handsome boyfriend like... like CJ Williams."

She imagined herself looking pretty like the white girls who lived closer to the city and went to the same school she did, at least when she actually went. She pictured her hair long and flowing over the back of her pink dress, which matched the pink socks folded neatly to kiss the top of her new black patent leather shoes, her wonderful, imaginary parents had bought for her. She imagined her mother and grandmother fussing over who would tie pink ribbons in her long hair before her imaginary boyfriend, CJ, came to take her out.

Her imaginary world offered an escape from reality. Her real world lacked white skin, long hair, black patent leather shoes, a new dress, caring parents, or a boyfriend.

Her second encounter with CJ resulted in her pregnancy. The bullies ambushed her while she was walking home from the store, calling her Aunt Jemima and throwing mud pancakes at her. She dropped her package and bent down to pick it up when a mud pancake hit her in the face. Her eyes and God's eyes released a flood of tears. Rain and tears blurred her vision, so she didn't see the fight start. CJ was wailing away at the boy who hit her with the mud. When the other one jumped in, CJ kept pounding and kicking both of them. God shed more tears, causing the two bullies to retreat, threatening to beat the shit out of CJ and her the next time.

"You okay?" CJ asked.

"Yes. Thank you. I..."

"They're NOT ever going to bother you again," he said with

finality. "Here," he said, handing her his coat. I'll walk you home. You can wear my coat 'til we get there."

I kin make it. Y'all don't need to do me no favors!" Evelyn said through tears. He felt sorry for her. Why else would he offer to give her his coat and walk her home? No sir! Evelyn wasn't going to let nobody, especially CJ Williams, feel sorry for her.

"I kin make it," she repeated. As if he hadn't heard her, CJ draped his jacket over her shoulders. After grabbing the bottle of Frank's Red Hot Sauce, the half-pound of lard wrapped in muddy white waxed paper, and the two-pound bag of Gold Medal flour, covered with dirt and water so that only the letters "Go dal" were visible, CJ kept walking beside her as they neared the outskirts of town.

Light had fallen on her corners. Evelyn's boyfriend, CJ Williams, was walking her home. She decided to let him kiss her goodnight on the front porch, just like Rhett Butler kissed Scarlett O'Hara in *Gone With The Wind*, the only movie Evelyn had ever seen.

She imagined that both her parents, not just her grandmother with whom she shared a miserable life, would be waiting for them. Her imaginary father would talk to the young man about his intentions while her imaginary mother offered them tea and cookies.

When they arrived at the little shack Evelyn called home,

reality overtook imagination. She took off his coat and tried to take the package from him before he could enter the house.

"I kin make it the rest of the way. Thank you for everythang," she averted CJ's eyes, certain they could pierce the shadows and see into her soul.

"Lemme carry it in for you." Without waiting for a response, CJ headed for the door and walked in. Evelyn's imagination couldn't change the scene CJ's eyes witnessed. A single kerosene lamp lit the room. The marvel of electricity hadn't yet reached many parts of rural Ohio. She hoped that the lack of faucets on the sink, indicating no running water, would go unnoticed by him. Evelyn was sure CJ had never seen people living in conditions like this, although everybody in town seemed to know about families like hers who squatted in shacks on the city's fringe.

The stench from the slop jar in the corner overpowered the aroma of her grandmother's fried chicken, greens, and cornbread supper, greeting them as they entered the tiny shack.

CJ quickly placed the package on the table and turned to leave, but hesitated. Light from the kerosene lamp danced on Evelyn's mud-stained face, capturing an image filled with shame in her eyes. Rain and mud molded the thin fabric of her dress to her body, revealing her developing breasts and rounded hips while outlining the V-shape between her thighs. She was no longer the smelly little girl that CJ helped that night or six weeks earlier.

Evelyn couldn't read CJ's mind, so she let her imagination take over. Her boyfriend had traveled all this way to see her, and she was enjoying his company. He was there in her parlor, and she was incredibly grateful. On the wooden table between the kerosene lamp and the remnants of the store package he helped carry in, Evelyn showed CJ just how thankful she was. She wasn't imagining this feeling; her boyfriend was kissing her and loving her—not on the hard, wooden table in the kitchen, but in that beautiful downtown hotel where she was sure the white girls and their boyfriends went. God had answered her prayers. She prayed it would never end.

When she felt his body tremble and heard his breathing return to normal, she knew it was over. Had Evelyn suspected that Gram was silently witnessing their union from behind the curtain that separated the bedroom from the rest of the shack, she would have run away never to be seen again.

"Those boys been bothering you in other ways?" CJ asked, recovering from the brief but satisfying embrace. "I can tell. I wasn't the first."

"No, no," she stammered, "Tweren't no boys."

CJ looked at this pitiful child; she couldn't have been more than thirteen and felt instant remorse for what he had done. He was a man, and she was a kid.

"Who?" Neither of them knew her grandmother was watching the entire scene from the next room, spit can in hand. Sounds of movement from the bedroom caused Evelyn to say, "leave, please, jes leave."

CJ hesitated, then turned and walked out the door. It was two weeks before she saw him again.

"Who?" The question startled Evelyn. She turned and saw CJ.

"Who?" he repeated.

Evelyn lowered her head and whispered, "Granddaddy."

When Evelyn's blood flow was replaced by violent morning sickness, her grandmother knew.

"Now, you's ruint." Evelyn was startled by her grandmother's voice, but she could not stop retching the contents of her stomach while holding her head out the door.

"Ain't no man gon' want you now. I's all ya'll got." Spit. "I gon' take care of you now. . . then ya'll gots to take care of me." Evelyn's sin was that her grandmother had an insurance policy for which deposits were regularly collected.

Despite her daughter's protests, Gram kept Evelyn inside the tiny shack until the baby was born, preventing her from breathing in the sweet smells of spring or turning her face to the summer sunshine.

"Ya'll's a disgrace," Gram told her. "Messing with your own. Ain't no good come of you naw, that bastard child."

Evelyn knew her grandmother believed her husband, Evelyn's step-grandfather, might be responsible for the baby growing inside her. Although Gram had seen the young man and her in the kitchen, she still blamed Evelyn and her unborn child for her lonely bed.

What had Gram told her, "He ain't hurt you none. Why you always gotsta fight?" So hurt by this question, Evelyn ignored it. All she could think about was that her grandmother knew what he was doing and did nothing to stop it. She wondered if her mother also knew.

On the morning after her son was born, Evelyn found a brown paper bag containing six cloth diapers, one Evenflow glass baby bottle, a quart of Isley's milk, and a sky-blue knit hat for the baby. Over the years, the packages kept coming. Sometimes, there was money, but mostly, they contained things for her son. Gram said that the packages were proof of what a good man Evelyn had driven away. Evelyn, on the other hand, believed the gifts were proof that Gram would not recognize a good man even if she saw one.

Chapter 8

Frank

Ever since he could remember, Frank had to empty his great grandmother's spit can. It was his job, Evelyn told him. Everyone had to contribute to the household, and Frank's only job was to empty Greatgram's spit can three times a day. Frank hated the job.

"Can't I wash the dishes or sweep the floor or do something else 'sides empty that nasty old can? Why can't that evil old woman empty her own can?"

Evelyn stopped in the middle of her cleaning. She grabbed Frank by the shirt collar and drew him close to her. Frightened by the look on his mother's face, he said nothing.

"Now you see here, Mista Franklin Harold Evans. Your great-grandmother wasn't too high and mighty to wash the shit from your body when you weren't more 'an knee high to a cat. That woman you call evil took care of you and me and Momma when we had nobody. Now all she asks you to do is to take your narrow ass into her room and empty her spit can. It ain't too much to ax, and you gonna do it."

Hard work gave Evelyn the means to support herself, her mother, her son, and her grandmother. Although childhood memories of her grandmother were anything but pleasant, Evelyn cared for the old woman as a dutiful servant cares for a tyrannical master—providing needed services while withholding any emotional connection. Silently, she marveled at how her son, Frank, a mere child, could stand up to Greatgram, something Evelyn could never do. Evelyn understood why Frank hated his great-grandmother, recalling her own childhood under the rule of this mean, evil old woman—too lazy to do anything but cook, eat, dip that nasty snuff, and order them around, especially Frank.

The tears flowing from Frank's eyes caused Evelyn to mellow just as he knew she would. "Franklin, without your great-grandmother, I don't know how we would have made it. Momma had to clean Ms Jessup's house and take care of her kids. I was jes a child myself. Without Greatgram… Jes, do it for me, please, honey."

Holding his nose and averting his eyes, Frank obeyed his mother's wishes until... It was Easter Sunday, and he and Evelyn always attended church together on that day. She bought new clothes for both of them, and Frank always felt special.

Five minutes after they returned from church, he heard the familiar request coming from his great-grandmother's room. "Frankie, come empty dis here can."

He hesitated for a moment, wondering whether he should change clothes. No, he decided, he wanted Greatgram to see him all dressed up.

"She did it on purpose!" Frank shouted to Evelyn between tears and sobs. "She put that nasty old can right in front of the door so I would trip over it. I hate her!" Frank's blue suit, covered with streaks of brown slime, a mixture of saliva and tobacco juice, made Evelyn's eyes water.

"Don't worry, baby, I can clean it. It'll look just like new." His mother's reassurance didn't convince him, and probably didn't convince her.

"She did it on purpose!" Frank stammered. "I ain't gonna do it no more. I mean it. I ain't never ever touching Greatgram's nasty old can ever again."

Frank successfully avoided the task when his mother was nearby. He enjoyed watching his great-grandmother empty her own can with a smug sense of satisfaction. But he knew it wasn't over.

"C'mer boy. Empty dis here spit can for your ole granny," she demanded of Frank about a week after the suit incident. Evelyn was gone and just the two of them were in the house. Only the sight and stench of the contents in what she referred to as her spit can superseded Frank's revulsion at the brown liquid trickling down her chin as she spoke. He looked directly into those hollow, glazed eyes and challenged her.

"No!" Seven-year-old Frank mustered the will to say, "I ain't gonna empty that nasty can no more." Greatgram was a full-sized woman. Frank marveled at how she could maneuver all of that weight. He waited as she lowered her bulk into the closest, sturdiest chair. Sweating by this time, she balanced the spit can on the triangle her dress formed when stretched beneath folds of stomach fat and over thighs heading in opposite directions.

"You empty dis here can or God's goin' make yo water run!"

Her threat triggered nightly dreams of running water, leaking faucets, flowing rivers, and raging waterfalls. Water was everywhere in different forms, causing the urge to relieve his bladder.

"You too old to be peeing the bed, Franklin! And I ain't got time to be washing these sheets every day! What's come over you?" Evelyn was beside herself with frustration about her son's recent bladder control problem.

"Greatgram did it!" was all Frank could say. Greatgram had cursed him. Why else did he keep having strange dreams at night, filled with flowing water? There was a never-ending faucet that he couldn't turn off, tons of water rushing over waterfalls, and a swimming pool that kept filling up with more and more water, with Frank swirling in the middle. Water. Water. Water. It had to be Greatgram's doing. But he had decided that he would never touch that can again.

His mother scolded him, and his schoolmates teased him

because of the pee smell. With no other option, Frank pinched his nose, breathed through his mouth, held the can at arm's length, and poured it into their newly installed toilet. Greatgram became even more demanding, but at least the strange dreams and the peeing had stopped.

"Fetch me some cold watta, boy. Put two pieces of ice in it. That's all," Greatgram would say. With the toilet, running water was also added to the house. If Frank hesitated, she'd warn him, "If you don't do what Ah say, the Lord'll punish you."

The smell of the Railroad Mill Snuff stuck between her lower lip and her few remaining brown teeth made her breath smell awful. Frank patiently waited for her to finish before taking a breath himself. He returned with a glass of water containing two ice cubes, thinking about the consequences of disobeying his great-grandmother and refusing to go near that can.

Suddenly, the sound of breaking glass grabbed his attention, and he hurried to the kitchen just in time to see his mother cleaning up tomato juice and shattered glass from the floor.

"What happened?" a wide-eyed Frank asked.

"Momma accidentally dropped the pitcher of tomato juice," she sighed. "Boy! What a mess! One good thing, though," his mother said, continuing to wipe at the running liquid, "I didn't spill it on the new carpet." His mother sighed again, still wiping at the spilled liquid.

A week passed before Frank accidentally spilled Greatgram's spit can on the new sky-blue wall-to-wall carpeting in the living room. He watched in dismay as the brown goo oozed out, moving slowly like thick molasses, forming a puddle that was greedily absorbed by the woolen fibers. Desperate, he called Evelyn, choking back sobs and tears, and repeatedly apologized as he explained how he had tripped on the plastic runner, causing the can's contents to spill.

Evelyn was horrified by the large brown stain on her brand-new carpet. She scrubbed vigorously until only a faint outline of the spill remained. Despite Frank's fake apologies and insincere pleas for another chance, Evelyn took charge of the task of emptying the can.

"You ain't fooling me none, boy," Greatgram said, spitting into the can. "I knows it wasn't no acceedent. You're just like your daddy." Spit. "You ain't gonna be nothing... nothing at all," she declared, her anger stopping just short of cursing him this time. Frank locked eyes with her, his voice firm, "I told you, and I told you! I wasn't gonna empty that nasty can no more. I don't care if you curse me again and make me burn myself up. I ain't doing it. Do you believe me now?"

It had been several years since Greatgram passed away, yet

she still held a grudge against her granddaughter for emptying her bed. Frank and Evelyn believed she had gone to a place they both thought she deserved.

At fifteen, Frank's true nature was impossible to hide. He had a tan complexion that looked great next to his gray-green eyes. His thick, curly hair was always neatly arranged, forming tight curls around a square face with a broad nose and thick eyebrows. His full lips seemed like they were permanently glossed. He was the spitting image of CJ Williams.

Frank's good looks made him an instant favorite among teachers, and students admired him. In return for their adoration, Frank tolerated teachers and found ways to exploit his popularity.

"All I do, Mom, is buy chips, gum, and candy bars from Jake's and sell them to the kids between classes. It's okay. The teachers don't mind," Frank explained. Evelyn accepted this explanation for the extra pocket change Frank always seemed to have. But when Frank's candy sales grew beyond what his locker could hold, he decided it was time to find a partner he could trust.

"Regis, man, you want to make some money?" Frank asked.

Regis raised an eyebrow, curious. "What do I have to do?"

"Nothing, man, just let me use your locker," Frank said as he handed Regis a Snickers bar, which Regis promptly accepted.

Regis squinted, trying to figure out Frank's plan. "What's it for?"

Frank waved off the question with feigned frustration and anger. "Never mind," he replied. "I'll let someone else do it!"

"Okay," Regis said, agreeing without fully knowing what he was getting into.

Frank pressed, "Okay, what?"

Regis sighed and relented, "You can use my locker."

If anyone could be bought as a friend, it was Regis Burns. Frank jokingly told his friends that Regis cost him just one Snickers bar, and he was still waiting for his change. Frank was careful not to let their friendship become too public, as winners never hung out with losers. However, behind closed doors, the two were indeed friends. Regis enjoyed the times at Frank's house, where he could ogle Frank's girlie magazines, while Frank counted the money Regis had made from that day's sales. Observing the two together, Evelyn sensed that Regis, like herself, lived in the shadows.

Evelyn liked Regis and was surprised that her son had befriended him. Poverty alone was enough to make Regis an outcast, but his lack of intelligence, large lips, and unappealing odor made him unpopular with both teachers and classmates. Frank's motives for befriending Regis were a mystery to Evelyn. Despite her doubts, she had grown to like the boy, a feeling that remained even after Frank and Regis were no longer friends. "How come Regis don't come 'round here no more?" Evelyn asked Frank. Frank knew that his mother had developed a fondness for Regis. How his mother could care for someone who seems to live in shadows was beyond Frank's comprehension. But he was not surprised by her question. He had rehearsed his answer for weeks.

"He got kicked out of school," Frank replied.

Evelyn's eyes widened with concern. "Why? What happened?"

Frank hesitated briefly before answering, "He stole the teacher's wallet." Evelyn felt a mix of relief that her son was doing well in school and concern about Regis's actions. What Evelyn didn't realize was that Frank was using money from his candy-selling business to boost his grades. He traded candy for used homework papers, bought exam answers from the teacher's pets, and even bribed students to steal grade books when his C's outnumbered his A's.

Frank had managed to manipulate his grades to maintain a B average before the final math exam, even though he didn't really expect to pass it. If he didn't come up with a clever plan quickly, he would have to face Miss Norris's exam completely unprepared. "Franklin, you know I think you are one of my best students, don't you?" Miss Norris asked.

He hated it when teachers called him Franklin. "Yes, Miss Norris," he replied.

"Now, Franklin, I want you to tell me the truth. You will not be punished if you just tell the truth. Do you understand?"

"Yes, Miss Norris," Frank replied.

"Do you know who stole my wallet?" Miss Norris inquired. Frank decided to play along and mimicked the behavior of the kids he called suck-ups, the teacher pleasers. He contorted his face into a sad, about-to-cry expression, lowered his eyes, and dropped his head.

Miss Norris placed her hand under his chin and raised his head.

It had taken all his strength, but his eyes now contained enough water to make sorrowful tears flow. "Y.. y.. yes," he barely whispered.

"Who stole the wallet, Franklin?" Miss Norris persisted.

Frank pressed on with his act, begging, "Please don't... please don't make me tell, Miss Norris." "Franklin, we don't help our friends by lying for them; we only help them when we tell the truth. Was it Regis Burns? Did Regis steal my wallet?"

Frank maintained his facade and said, "Yes, Ma'am... Regis

stole it."

Regis was expelled after Miss Norris's wallet was found in his locker, along with a few candy bars reported missing from the cafeteria.

It had cost Frank a lot to have the wallet stolen and placed in Regis's locker, but the pride in Evelyn's eyes when he showed her his all A's report card made it worth every penny. Evelyn was truly proud of her son. Frank didn't have to live in an imagined world like her and Regis; he shaped his reality according to his desires.

To keep his mother proud, Frank began attending church with her regularly. However, Evelyn suspected that his newfound religious commitment had little to do with a genuine desire to serve God. Based on how much time he spent staring at Paula Shannon, the Pastor's daughter, Evelyn believed there were other motives involved.

Why Frank was attracted to Paula remained a mystery to Evelyn and the other churchgoers. Paula was dark-skinned, had short hair, and crooked teeth. Her bony frame was not particularly sexy, except for one feature. God had blessed her with the fullest, high-riding butt ever bestowed on one of His displaced children. It was a magnet, and Frank was caught.

Evelyn called it courting, but Frank knew it was more like seduction. He prepared for this stage of his plan by reading select

Bible passages and memorizing key verses from each of the sixty-six books. In just three months, Frank had confessed his sins, been baptized, and become a respected youth member of the Greater Mt. Sinai Community Missionary Baptist Church.

Evelyn and Mrs. Shannon, Paula's mother, became close friends, and their families often visited each other. Reverend Shannon, convinced that Frank had honorable intentions, allowed Paula to begin dating him.

Their sexual relationship began on a rainy night, with raindrops pattering on Frank's bedroom window. It abruptly ended when Paula revealed she was pregnant. An argument broke out when Frank told his mother the news, causing Evelyn to realize she didn't truly know her son.

"Paula's a nice girl, Franklin," Evelyn began, trying to find a solution. "You can live right here with me after you're married. Greatgram's old room would..."

"I am NOT marrying Paula!" The finality in his voice reminded her of CJ's words to her, 'Those boys will never bother you again,' so she quickly changed the subject.

"What are you going to do about that baby?" she asked.

"Nothing! I grew up without a father, and I'm doing just fine," Frank retorted defensively. "Paula's baby can do the same.

Hell, I ain't never even seen my daddy." His last words cut through the air, piercing Evelyn's heart. For the first time, she felt deep shame for her only son and herself.

"Franklin, don't let what happened to me and you happen to Paula and your baby," Evelyn pleaded, hoping he would reconsider.

Frank exploded in anger, his words sharp and painful, "You're going to be just like your daddy. He wasn't nothing, and you ain't going to be nothing. You're just like him." His bitter words echoed the hurtful things Greatgram had said about his absent father, casting a dark shadow over their strained relationship for the rest of his life.

Chapter 9

Mirembee and Louise

Mirembee, at eighteen years old, had a rather plain appearance mainly due to her clothing and grooming choices rather than a lack of natural beauty. Working as a waitress in a dead-end job, she managed to get her own apartment. Louise still helped with the bills since Mirembee's paycheck and tips couldn't cover all the monthly expenses. Mirembee saw this financial support as a small price to pay for letting Louise forget about her daughter's existence. CJ occasionally contributed as well, doing his best, and Mirembee loved him for it.

With these three sources of support, Mirembee managed to make ends meet.

After moving out of Louise's house, Mirembee stopped taking the birth control pills that Louise had insisted she take every morning. "Your control over me is over," Mirembee said as she flushed the remaining pills down the toilet.

When CJ died, the roll of bills in his pocket was worth less than fifty dollars. The police gave the money and a set of keys, which were also found on his body, to Mirembee. He had very few other assets, which put Mirembee in the awkward position of asking Louise for money to cover his burial. Louise could afford a nice funeral for CJ, and she owed him that much, Mirembee thought. Of course, her other option was for the county to bury him in a cardboard box and leave his body among the John and Jane Does dumped in the pauper cemetery. The welfare department or Louise, Mirembee considered. Damn!

"Louise," she said firmly, "I need help with the funeral costs." Since Mirembee now goes by Rembee, she called her mother Louise.

"What do you mean? I'm sure your father had some form of insurance, Mirembee!" Louise lied.

"No, he... will you help me bury Daddy?" Mirembee, using all her self-control, avoided getting into an argument. "The funeral costs five thousand dollars." Though this amount felt staggering to Mirembee, it was only a down payment for a new car or another mink coat for Louise. Mirembee took in a deep breath.

Mirembee, like Louise, realized that money wasn't the main issue. They never truly understood each other's perspectives. Louise had constantly given Mirembee material things, even now helping cover some of her monthly expenses. But what Mirembee really wanted was a mother's love and the financial support to give her father a proper burial – something Louise was unwilling to do.

It's because she has his eyes," Louise once told Lee, making the connection even though she knew it wasn't scientifically backed.

"Those damn gray/green eyes." Thoughts of those eyes, which once looked so deeply from the now-deceased CJ, caused Louise to soften just a little, as she briefly revisited long nights spent gazing into those eyes.

"I'll give you two thousand, and not a cent more. He can have a decent burial for two thousand dollars." Louise knew, and Mirembee knew as well, that Louise could have easily provided the extra three thousand. However, Louise felt compelled to remind Mirembee that it was her mother, not her father, who had supported them when CJ was alive and continued to do so even in his passing.

Mirembee needed Louise.

"Louise, I need five-thousand. If you can't. . . won't give it to me, I'll ask Lee."

"Don't you dare!" Louise screamed furiously. "Don't you dare bring Lee into this!" Louise, no longer in control of her anger, lashed out at her daughter. "Isn't it enough that Lee's money pays your bills every month? Now you want him to bury that good-for-nothing piece of..." Louise stopped, regaining control. "Lee will not give you a dime unless I tell him to. You know it! Take the two thousand before I change my mind, Mirembee Sophia." "Using Mirembee's full name was Louise's way of concluding their unpleasant conversations. In the ongoing battle of wills, the victor remained the same, but this time, the victim had stood up, attempted to defend herself, and reacted. Mirembee was claiming a second chance at life.",

"Thank you, Mother," Mirembee said in her most subservient, sarcastic tone. She waited patiently as Louise's trembling right hand wrote the check. The signed check was thrust at Mirembee as she turned to leave. The soft sound of her shoes stopped as she reached the foyer door.

"Goodbye, Louise," Mirembee said, turning toward the woman who had given her birth and looking her straight in the eyes. "Goodbye!"

Mirembee did not hate Louise. She had tried, really wanting to hate her mother. Right after the abortion, Mirembee had wished her dead. And not just any death, Mirembee told God. Make her suffer like my baby suffered. Every imaginable terrible death that Mirembee could think of, she wished upon Louise. A car accident with her mangled body unrecognizable. Death by fire in her burning house, gasping for air. An attacker with a long knife, hacked to death, dismembered. Images of blood and body parts haunted Mirembee most nights. The dreams did not bring tears. This was justifiable death, as Mirembee saw it.

Separation made her see Louise differently. Louise, Mirembee decided, was a very pathetic person—like Sisyphus condemned by Zeus to push a stone up the hill only to have it fall back again and again. Then he would have to start over, pushing that stone up once more. Louise pushed her stone of materialism only to find it was never enough; the next day, it all started over again.

When Louise acquired a half-carat diamond, she would invariably covet a full carat. She constantly longed for more, more of everything except love. Louise was neither the recipient nor the giver of love. This realization freed Mirembee from her hatred, but instead of feeling relief, she was overwhelmed by a deep sense of emptiness.

Mirembee learned the secret to surviving with Louise: keep a spotless house, praise her latest purchases, and never ask for more money than Louise is willing to give. But whether Louise was willing or not, Mirembee needed the money to give CJ a proper burial, a tribute to his most cherished possession—his pride. She couldn't bear the thought of letting him lose in death what he had worked so hard for in life, limited by a mere two-hundred-dollar allowance from the county. She resolved to find the extra three thousand dollars somehow and vowed never to accept another penny from Louise for as long as she lived.

Chapter 10

Elijah C.J. Alonso Patrick

Elijah's name was a misnomer. In the Bible, Elijah was a prophet who delivered good news. Elijah CJ Alonzo Patrick, however, was more like a bearer of bad news. Like the bag lady who picks up cast-offs from other people's lives, Elijah collected discarded bits and pieces of life itself.

From birth, Elijah proved to be a difficult child. CJ blamed his mother for it. The relationship that resulted in Elijah's birth happened when CJ was still young, and Elijah's mother was only sixteen and known for her wild behavior.

CJ knew he wasn't the only boy to spend the fifteen minutes with Lucy that resulted in her pregnancy. However, when he saw this light-skinned baby with gray-green eyes, he realized it was his child.

Elijah was CJ's second child. CJ never understood why Evelyn's grandmother insisted that he was not Franklin's father. He had no doubt about his paternity. Although he couldn't be as involved in Franklin's life, aside from occasional small gifts and the money he left at Evelyn's door, CJ was determined to be an active part of Elijah's life. He steadfastly refused to abandon the child and his mother, despite the sneers and advice from his friends to do so.

Heroin sneaked into Cleveland like a thief, robbing Black folks of their humanity. It wasn't long before Elijah's mother became a victim and abandoned CJ and her child. She was there physically, but the poison injected into her veins each morning and night consumed her mind, body, and soul. Lucy Patrick was just one more victim whose life would slowly be taken and forgotten.

Her habit brought drugs and babies into the home where Elijah spent his early years. From a young age, Elijah learned the tough realities of surviving. He disliked the men his momma brought home, so he didn't mind doing exactly what she told him—going through their pockets and taking money while she entertained them in the bedroom. She showed him to take just enough for food, save a little for her, and leave most so the men wouldn't get suspicious or wouldn't care. If they did notice missing money, the larger bills stayed, so it wasn't worth the trouble to retrieve what was taken.

When he was eight years old, the heavyset man who came home with his momma had no change, just a fifty-dollar bill. Elijah was hungry, as were his brothers and sister. He took the money, knowing he'd face his momma's disapproval.

As he approached the apartment door, Elijah heard the yelling and arguing from inside. Brown paper bags with "KROGER" written in the blue oval, filled with groceries, were too important to drop, so he clung tightly to them and rushed into the apartment.

"Lijah, Lijah, he hurtin' momma!" Wide-eyed, his brothers and sister turned to eight-year-old Elijah, hoping he could do something to stop the beating. Elijah quickly gathered the kids and hid the bags of food behind the worn sofa, which was propped up on one end by two red bricks. Food was a matter of survival, and he was determined not to lose those bags if he could help it. Elijah guided his brothers and sister into their shared bedroom, telling them to lock the door and not open it unless he said so.

"Lijah, make him stop hurtin momma. Please Lijah," his sister said, "don't let him hurt momma no more."

The big man was screaming. "What the fuck you do with my money, bitch?" Folds of black fat and the largest dick Elijah has ever seen stood bending over the sobbing, bloody shadow that was his mother. The hairy back, shoulders so broad that his arms hung away from his body, reminded Elijah of the nature films all the boys at school liked to watch. Elijah had to challenge Alpha Gorilla, the biggest, baddest male in the troop, to save his mother. The gorilla struck Lucy hard in the face. Blood splattered; a tooth flew out of her mouth. Elijah, like one of the big cats in those films, leapt onto the gorilla's back, kicking, hitting, and biting.

"Fucker, let my momma go!" he shouted. Like a dog shaking off water, the gorilla shook himself effortlessly until Elijah was thrown onto the sagging middle of the bed. Then, with his attention returning to the woman on the floor, the gorilla delivered a brutal kick to her stomach, causing more blood to spurt from her mouth.

"I want my money now!" the gorilla roared in a fit of rage. Elijah half-expected the gorilla to start beating his chest like a primal beast. But instead, another merciless kick landed, causing more blood to flow. Elijah, desperate, scanned the room for something, anything, to stop this gorilla from killing his mother. He seized Lucy's prized gold-colored lamp, a rescued treasure from the weekly trash pickup. Swiftly, he removed the red velvet shade and jammed the still-burning light bulb into the gorilla's bare back until the lamp began to pop and crackle, leaving small shards of glass embedded in the gorilla's flesh. The gorilla howled, spun around, and fixed his narrowed eyes on Elijah.

Elijah's reflexes were lightning-fast. He executed a backflip across the bed and landed on the floor just as the massive hand grabbed his shirt. In seconds, Elijah wriggled out of his shirt and crawled under the bed to the other side, scraping his head and back on loose springs from the well-used bed. The blood from the scratches didn't stop him. Elijah made a beeline for the bathroom, slamming the door with the gorilla hot on his heels. Like all jungle predators, proud of their size, the gorilla pursued his prey with relentless determination. Underestimating his opponent, he swung the bathroom door open to find Elijah poised with a can of hairspray, ready and waiting.

Elijah aimed for the eyes and the hairy chest, spraying as hard as he could to force the gorilla to retreat. Being wounded only makes animals angrier and more aggressive, but it rarely stops them. The gorilla wiped his eyes, gaining just enough vision to see his target and lunge at him once more. Too little, too late. Brains beat brawn. The lit match in Elijah's hand was already headed toward the gorilla's chest as the police burst through the front door.

His brothers and sister were sent to foster homes, while Elijah was placed in a state youth facility. Despite his young age, the court decided that the violent nature of his actions required rehabilitation through the juvenile justice system instead of the child protective services.

Elijah didn't particularly mind the institution. He had a comfortable place to sleep and got three meals a day. His duties included going to school and keeping his room tidy, while the older kids handled the tougher tasks. Elijah felt he had it pretty good, but he couldn't help missing his momma and worrying about whether his brothers and sister were getting proper care. Sometimes, his dad came to visit him, promising him a home as soon as he was released.

Elijah, accustomed to his dad's promises thought that is all they are, promises.

"You are going home today, Elijah," the superintendent announced unceremoniously.

"Home," Elijah said excitedly. "Is my mother here?"

"No," he said, "your father."

Elijah said nothing to CJ until the car stopped and they were seated in front of what had once been a single-family home, but now accommodated four families in the same space.

"Where is my mother?" Elijah asked.

"Son. . . ."

"Don't call me that! My name is Elijah!"

"I know your name." I named you boy." CJ boomed out an abbreviated version of Malachi 4:5-6: 'Behold, I will send you Elijah the prophet... and he shall turn the hearts of the fathers to the children, and the hearts of the children to their fathers... ' I am your father!"

"Says you."

CJ felt the urge to hit his son, but he managed to restrain himself. "Your mother's sick, son," he said, his voice trembling with emotion. "She's in a hospital, and they're going to try to help her get better. In the meantime, you're going to live with me."

Elijah looked up with concern. "What about my sister and brothers? Are they coming too?"

CJ shook his head sadly. "No, they won't be coming with us, but they're in a good foster home where they'll be taken care of."

"I'm supposed to take care of them," Elijah said with a heavy heart.

Elijah tried to wipe away the tears that were escaping from the corners of his eyes with the back of his hand. CJ pretended not to notice.

Father and son got out of the car and walked into the old dining room, which had been turned into an efficiency apartment.

Over the next six months, a power struggle unfolded between them. Sometimes, the conflict was like a cold war, with tensions simmering just below the surface. Other times, it turned into a fierce fight where neither side held back. Whether the battles were hot or cold, CJ always emerged as the victor.

War or peace, Elijah began to develop a respect for his father. He admired CJ's skills and abilities. CJ had a talent for bringing home broken electrical appliances like toasters, radios, and even televisions, then repairing them to work as good as new. At first, he let Elijah watch him work, but soon, Elijah became his unofficial apprentice. As they delved into the intricacies of electric circuitry, CJ discovered that not only was his son a quick learner, but he also had a natural talent for using his hands.

Their home in Cleveland's East Side neighborhood attracted a steady stream of customers who found their way to CJ's door. Elijah wasn't entirely sure if they were there to buy something or just to sit and listen to the stories CJ shared. CJ's habit of talking about inventing something big and making a fortune caught their attention. Elijah wasn't sure if the customers believed in CJ's dream, but he knew his father was convinced it could happen.

Elijah was reluctant to leave when CJ shared the news that Lucy was better and had a home ready for Elijah, his brothers, and his sister.

"You have to go, son. Your mother needs you," CJ explained.

"But I want to stay with you," Elijah pleaded earnestly. "I can help you fix things. I know how. Please, CJ, let me stay. I won't be no trouble." Neither tears nor begging changed CJ's mind.

"It ain't up to me, son," CJ said, his voice cracking as he fought back tears. "The county says you've got to be with your mother. Besides, Lucy needs you." CJ's mind flashed back to the old cliché his own father had used while administering discipline with a belt: "This hurts me more than it hurts you." CJ had come to terms with this father-and-son arrangement as his new reality. He found solace in having one of his children with him and took pride in sharing his dreams and teaching Elijah the intricacies of electric circuitry. He did not want his son to leave, but he felt he had no choice.

Lucy managed to stay clean for about six months after Elijah was returned home. During that time, their living conditions were the best that twelve-year-old Elijah could remember. Until that day when he came home from school greeted by the sickening sight of his mother lying in bed, her gaze fixed on the TV, and a cigarette burning a hole in the carpet. Elijah hurriedly put out the cigarette.

After preparing dinner, including a hot dog and two cans of Chef Boyardee spaghetti for his brothers and sister, such as his new little sister and brother—twins, Lucy added while he was living with CJ—he then took a tray of hot Campbell Tomato Soup, some crackers, and grape Kool-Aid to his mother bedside.

"I love you, baby," she slurred. "You sho do take care of yo momma."

"I love you too, Momma," Elijah said, his voice filled with both love and concern. After leaving his mother's room, he stepped away to a spot out of sight of his sisters and brothers, where he could let his tears flow freely. Over the next six months, things continued to get worse. Elijah saw his father less and less. Elijah heard that CJ had gotten married and had a daughter, and he guessed that this new family might be the reason CJ didn't visit as often anymore.

Although he skipped school, he made sure the other kids went regularly. Every morning, he got up, fixed breakfast for his brothers and sisters, and helped dress them for school. Afterwards, he would wait to see what his mother was going to do. Some days, she went out. Some days, men came to the house. If she looked capable of taking care of the babies, Elijah would leave the house to find some quick work so he could earn some pocket change.

Their monthly welfare check barely covered their basic needs, let alone the costs of his mother's drug habit. Lucy turned to the only means she knew to supplement their income. Elijah initially managed to get some money from CJ, but that changed when CJ started asking too many questions. Elijah kept up the pretense that everything was fine, and CJ, avoiding the house, never saw their dire living conditions. All the furniture, except for two beds and an old, worn-out couch, was gone. By the end of the month, the refrigerator and cupboards were empty.

During his last visit, CJ gave his son twenty dollars and left. It would be five long years before they saw each other again.

Twenty dollars wasn't nearly enough to buy the food Elijah and his family needed, so he paid for what he could and discreetly stole the rest, hiding it under his jacket. Unfortunately, security guards caught him just outside the store and immediately called the police. The police, upon seeing the deplorable conditions of Lucy's home, contacted the welfare department. The younger children were returned to foster care, while Elijah was sent to a youth camp in upstate New York.

CJ tried to find him, but even though Elijah had lived with CJ for a year, there was no proof that he was Elijah's father. The bureaucrats refused to give CJ any information about his son's whereabouts.

Five years later, at eighteen, Elijah left the youth camp. His momma had passed away, officially from pneumonia, but Elijah knew the real reason behind her death. Heroin and gorillas had taken her from him. His sisters and brothers had all been adopted or placed in foster homes, and the records were sealed, according to the young white caseworker who seemed only a few years older than Elijah. She expressed her regret but explained that she couldn't provide any information about the children who shared his blood.

With all the sincerity of her Bachelor of Arts degree, she advised Elijah to find a job and become a responsible citizen. Only CJ remained. Elijah couldn't muster the motivation to search for his father. After all, CJ hadn't tried to find him all these years, thought Elijah.

Elijah tried to straighten out his life for a while, taking odd jobs to make ends meet. On Friday and Saturday nights, he often found himself at the bar, indulging in a little too much drinking but otherwise enjoying harmless revelry. Things weren't great, but they weren't terrible either. Elijah's lack of a clear direction didn't bother him; he was content with the present, and that was what mattered.

The assault on the man in the bar landed him with another ten years, this time in prison. When the judge asked him why he had broken the beer bottle over the man's head and shoved the skinny end up the man's ass, Elijah replied, "He tried to sell me heroin, and I wanted to show him what he could do with it."

Elijah spent the next five years moving in and out of various correctional facilities. Despite his efforts, he couldn't find his sisters and brothers, but he had managed to locate his father and occasionally exchange letters with him.

His release from prison came unexpectedly, thanks to a new Ohio law called Shock Probation. Elijah found himself back in his old neighborhood. Within an hour of his release, he sat alone in a small diner, savoring the fried eggs, bacon, and grits special that the city code considered a restaurant meal. While scanning the newspaper for an affordable room to rent that wouldn't drain all of the $200 the state had given him, his eyes landed on a familiar name in the obituaries: Clarence James Williams. The funeral was scheduled for that afternoon. Elijah decided to attend his father's funeral.

Chapter 11

CJ's Will

Mirembee believed her father could have become wealthy and famous because of his global accomplishments. But he wasn't. God had given him an unshakeable sense of pride, which might seem like a blessing, but for CJ, it was more like a curse.

Mirembee heard her father say more than once, "I've never stolen, cheated, or harmed anyone. God's law and man's law are equal to me. I treat others as they treat me." The shame of being handcuffed in front of those who admired him and being taken to that dirty jail must have deeply saddened him, she concluded.

Her parents hadn't shared the same house for over five years, and they had been sleeping in the same bed only occasionally for nearly two years. Although her mother remarried two days after their divorce was finalized, Clarence seemed to drift through life, taking on various odd jobs, eating at McDonald's, and staying in different boarding houses after Louise kicked him out of their home. Mirembee knew her father's reputation for not holding steady employment. Louise often reminded them of this during their marriage. After the divorce, Mirembee was the sole recipient of Louise's criticisms of Clarence, which lessened but didn't completely stop until he got a job at Consolidated Electronics. Even

Mirembee was surprised that Consolidated was able to keep her father employed for almost five years. She was less surprised when she learned he left—not quit, just left.

Perhaps if he had stayed, Consolidated Electronics' benefits could have helped cover his funeral costs. But this wasn't the moment for wishful thinking or mourning his loss. Mirembee had to step up, take charge, and bury her father with the dignity he fought so hard to achieve in life.

Mirembee's father died a proud man, and that pride might have been what caused his death. During a dispute with the East Ohio Gas Company, CJ had refused to pay his bill.

"I am not stupid!" he yelled at the nondescript clerk. "It's your goddam billing department's fault. I'm not paying you one goddam cent more until you send me my refund and turn on my fucking heat." CJ thought if only this clerk had been a woman, he would get his refund and maybe a piece of ass too.

Instead, the clerk replied, "Your claim will be investigated, Mr. Williams. If we find that it is valid, a check will be mailed to you by our legal department within the next ninety days."

"Yeah," CJ snarled, "when I get my check, you will get yours."

CJ installed a small kerosene heater to fight off the cold that seeped through every crack in his rundown house. During a particularly cold spell in January's harsh Ohio winter, CJ turned the heater to its highest setting and went to bed. The bottle of black hair dye, which he used regularly after noticing the graying of his temples, was left uncapped near the heater. He might have survived if he had been sober, but he was battling old age, ghosts of his past, and, most importantly, even he was starting to doubt his dream.

CJ passed away when he realized he had few chances left to make his millions. Still, he held onto his vision, even if only barely. The substances in his body allowed him to stay in bed and breathe the toxic fumes until Clarence James Williams was no longer among the living.

Somewhat miraculously, Mirembee made a discovery that not only solved her immediate problem but also had a profound impact on the rest of her life.

After the police notified her that CJ Williams died from the fire at his house, Mirembee immediately headed to CJ's home. First, she needed to see the conditions in which her beloved father died. Second, she wanted and needed her father's car. While begging Louise to take her to the grocery store and waiting for the bus, Mirembee felt she wasn't in control of her destiny, at least not when it came to transportation. CJ's car could fix that. Finally, she wanted to inventory CJ's possessions before the leeches—who always hung around CJ begging for money—stripped the place clean. She needed to find out if CJ had any money or valuables left, especially an insurance policy to help cover his funeral costs. Using the keys the police had given her, she entered the house. The scavengers had come and eaten everything.

Unfortunately, there was no money or valuables left, only scattered papers and other junk strewn all over the floor. The papers seemed unharmed by the fire, leading Mirembee to deduce that they had been taken from a drawer or something similar by one of the scavengers searching for money. The rest of the house was covered in black soot and smoke. Mirembee spotted her father's handwriting on some papers, so she stooped down to carefully gather the letters and junk mail.

Mirembee took the papers to her father's car because the house was cold and dark. She quickly went through them one by one. Several were bills, and some she assumed had been paid because the return stubs were missing. There was an unopened letter from the gas company, which she believed was another bill, so she placed it in her purse. An open envelope with the name Elijah, without a last name in the upper left corner, caught her attention. She wasn't sure why, but she decided to keep it even though the envelope was empty. Another official-looking, legal-size envelope caught her eye. The address in the upper left corner read, "United States Patent and Trademark Office, 600 Dulany St, Alexandria, VA

22314." Inside was a packet containing diagrams and several pages of legal language, she thought. She made a mental note to examine the contents more closely later.

As she was about to toss the remaining stack, which she thought was junk mail, she remembered why she had picked up the papers in the first place – her father's handwriting was on one sheet of paper. She quickly sifted through the bills, junk mail, and political ads until she found what she was searching for. At first, she couldn't believe it. It was a handwritten will, or at least what she believed to be a will.

Why would CJ leave a will? Mirembee thought. For as long as she could remember, CJ never cared about material things. Instead, he lived a life denying himself common comforts like hot water, a flushing toilet, a bathtub, and a refrigerator that kept food cold.

His indifference to material things extended to his finances. Mirembee had some understanding of CJ's financial situation, or more accurately, his lack of funds. His estate mainly consisted of the now-charred house, which she estimated to be worth $10,000 at best before the fire. The house carried a $4,000 first mortgage and a $2,000 second mortgage. His well-worn Pontiac, the one she was currently sitting in, had an odometer nearing 200,000 miles but was free of any liens. Then there were his various odds and ends, what CJ always called his "stuff."

The will was dated three years earlier. Three years ago, five years after her abortion, and around the time Louise had him arrested for nonpayment of child support.

May 1, 1995

I, Clarence James Williams, also known as CJ, being of sound mind and body, do hereby give all my worldly possessions and the proceeds of my estate to my children. I trust my daughter, Mirembee Williams, to divide all monies, possessions, and properties equally among her sisters and brothers.

Frank Harold Evans
Jill
Elijah CJ Alonzo Patrick
Mirembee Pearl Williams
Jesse Williams Proctor
Carmen de Milo Bordeaux
CJ
Clarence James Williams
Annamay Grace Edmons
Ernest J. Knighten

"SISTERS AND BROTHERS!" The words leaped from the page, startling Mirembee. "Sisters! Brothers; Frank, Jill, Elijah." Her name was right after "Elijah." Frantically, Mirembee scoured the papers in search of the envelope with the name "Elijah" on it. However, her swift search yielded nothing. She returned to the will, where she reread the names: Mirembee, Jesse, Carmen. One, two, three, four, five, six. There were six names in total. Did this mean Mirembee Pearl Williams had two sisters and three brothers? Did her father list them in order of their age? Her own name fell in the middle. What significance did that hold? She read her father's words repeatedly, hoping that rereading them would somehow reveal more information.

Two names she didn't recognize, but suspected were some of the individuals she called "leeches," saw the will.

Chapter 12

Mirembee and Jesse

Sitting in the Pontiac, Mirembee was shocked after reading the will, questioning her feelings about her father, her mother, and herself. Did Louise know about the other children? It seemed unlikely, Mirembee thought, or she wouldn't have given her the check. Louise, being Louise, would have flaunted the others many times. Had her father remarried without telling her? Who were these mysterious sisters and brothers, and where were they?

Mirembee turned the key, but the Pontiac sputtered and refused to start. She tried again, this time pressing the gas pedal to the floor as CJ had taught her. The engine responded with a grinding noise but still didn't turn over. Mirembee rested her head against the steering wheel and wept for her lost baby, her mother's lack of love, and her now silent father. Her tears did not stop because her sorrow had vanished, but because she had given all she had. Like the last drop of toothpaste squeezed from an empty tube, there was nothing left. Nothing.

Mirembee tried the key again, and the engine burst, grinded, coughed, and finally sputtered to life, spewing enough gas to ignite. Remembering her driving lessons from CJ, she gently lifted her foot off the accelerator to let it rise slowly. The engine made a series of strange noises, but it eventually settled into an uneven hum. She waited a few more minutes, still not fully trusting CJ's only worldly possession, and then started her drive home.

As she drove, her thoughts fixated on the events of the past hour. She remembered the envelope with the name in the upper left corner. Wasn't the name "Elijah"? Part of her wanted to pull over and look for the envelope right then and there. But she worried that the car might not start again if she turned it off, so she decided to search for it when she could sit down with a clear head and think.

The telephone was ringing when Mirembee entered her small efficiency apartment. It was the place Louise had insisted she take after seeing the apartment Mirembee had originally chosen on the east side of Cleveland. "It's a damn rat hole," Louise shouted. "You can't live there."

Louise had found her a charming yellow apartment in Brooklyn Heights, which Mirembee affectionately called the "yellow garden" because of the quirky choice to paint all the walls yellow. Even the kitchen had yellow daisies wallpaper, and the bathroom wall was decorated with yellow daffodils, no matter the season.

Somehow, she wasn't surprised when she heard the voice on the other end identify himself as Jesse Proctor. Mirembee's world seemed to be slowly unraveling like a strand of yarn at the hem of a sweater.

"Hello Rembee. You don't know me, but I need to talk to you. It's very important," although she vaguely recognized the name from the list she'd found, it was his voice and the fact that he called her "Rembee" that made her accept the invitation. He sounded like her father.

Hesitatingly, Mirembee asked, "Are you my...? I mean, how do you know my name?"

"Please, just meet me. Give me five minutes of your time, please, please. It's about CJ."

He had called her Rembee and mentioned her father, CJ. "All right," Mirembee agreed. "When, where?"

"Now, at Marko's, the restaurant right around the corner from your place."

"I know where it is. I can be there in five minutes."

"Good," he said. "I'll see you then." Mirembee hung up, thinking, he knows where I live.

Mirembee entered the restaurant looking for her caller. "Rembee," he called out, "over here." Mirembee turned toward the man who seemed about her age, incredibly handsome, and clearly of mixed heritage. Their eyes met, and she felt a small sense of familiarity. "Rembee, please. Come here."

Mirembee joined him in the booth, and he immediately took her hand. It seemed like a natural gesture for him, as if he had known her all his life. But for Mirembee, it felt unnatural, and she instinctively pulled her hand away.

"My name is Mirembee!" she said, wondering why she had reverted to the name she had long abandoned, along with any claim that her birth was somehow connected with Louise's reproductive organs.

"I know your name, but CJ, our father, calls you… called you Rembee," Jesse said, his voice trembling with emotion. Mirembee could tell he had been crying. Now, tears flowed, and words became difficult.

"Our father?" Mirembee looked at him in astonishment. "Our father," she repeated, her voice barely a whisper. "Our father." This time, she repeated the words slowly and with a deep sense of realization. It was the beginning of a profound connection that would endure until death.

"Yes," Jesse affirmed, as if addressing the unspoken question. "I... I want to do something. I don't have much money, but I've been saving. Even my mother doesn't know how much money

I've got," he said quickly, faster than Mirembee's mind could keep up. "After all, he was my father, too. I just want to do something." "How much money do you have?" Mirembee's question was enough to shift their focus.

"A little over a thousand dollars," Jesse replied. Now, Mirembee's mind was racing. With the two thousand dollars Louise had given her and this extra thousand, she only needed another two thousand to give CJ a proper burial.

"Can you get more?" she pressed.

"I... don't know, I... could try. I..." It was clear to Mirembee that Jesse was struggling to come up with a thousand dollars, but she asked anyway.

"How soon can you get the money, the thousand?" she inquired.

"Today, I keep it hidden at the house."

"Good. You know where I live. Bring the money to my house. How long will it take you?",

"I can get the money and be over at your place by, say... one o'clock. I have to take the bus," Jesse said apologetically. He started to rise, eager to please his sister.

"Wait." Mirembee stopped him mid-rise. They hadn't ordered, but she took another sip of the hot coffee the waitress had poured after receiving an affirmative nod from Mirembee before continuing. "Did you know about the others?" "Others what?" Jesse, halfway out of his seat, responded with clear confusion. "The others!" Mirembee raised her voice, causing several restaurant patrons to turn in their direction. She lowered her voice, and Jesse sat back down. The server appeared and asked if they were ready to order. Mirembee waved her off and kept talking to Jesse. "CJ, our father, left a will." There, she had said it. "Our father." She acknowledged aloud what her mind hadn't fully accepted. She was glad she had the presence of mind to bring the will with her. She handed it to Jesse, who read it very slowly. When he finished, he looked up and gazed into his sister's eyes.

"I... knew about you. I've always known about you, Rembee, I mean Mirembee."

"It's okay, you can call me Rembee."

"But, I don't know nothing 'bout no other brothers or sisters. What are we going to do?" Jesse asked Mirembee, fully expecting that she would have an answer.

She looked at him and said, "We are going to get out of here."

Mirembee and Jesse walked the short distance to her apartment, aware that Jesse's eyes remained fixed on her. They waited until they were inside her apartment before delving into the will and discovering their father's other children. She showed him the envelope with the name "Elijah" on it, addressed to Clarence James Williams. There was no return address, but the back of the envelope bore a stamp that read, "INSPECTED FOR CONTENTS STATE OF OHIO DEPT. OF CORRECTIONS."

"What do you think he did?" Jesse asked.

"I... I don't know. How should I know?"

For the next five minutes, they speculated on the possible crimes that the brother they had never met might have committed.

"What if he killed somebody?"

"Try not to think the worst."

"Or robbed a bank?"

"Black people don't…" Mirembee stopped, sensing the mild disturbance in Jesse's face and silently acknowledging his obvious mixed parentage. "Tell me about your mother," she said.

They exchanged stories of their childhood, sharing humorous anecdotes about CJ's antics. Mirembee mostly listened as Jesse recounted his life growing up. She marveled as Jesse named each of the brothers and sisters he had lived with, their ages, their fathers, and what they were doing now, seemingly without taking a breath or hesitating before moving on to the next topic. Mirembee sat in silence, listening to Jesse. The evident love Jesse felt for his mother ignited a longing in her. A mother who genuinely loved her children and didn't harm unwanted babies was a treasure only the fortunate discovered at the end of the rainbow. Mirembee chose not to reveal much about herself or Louise. Besides, Jesse already seemed to know a lot about her. She directed her part of the conversation toward stories about CJ and his inventions.

As dawn broke and sunlight started filtering into the room, Jesse expressed his exhaustion and need for sleep. Mirembee refused, saying he had to get the money first. They were planning to give their father a proper burial. Jesse left the apartment driving the Pontiac, which he managed to start by connecting a loose wire to the spark plug. Little did they know, it would be the last time he would leave Mirembee's side.

Chapter 13
Attorney Stock

With Jesse gone, Mirembee, fueled by adrenaline, began sorting through and organizing the papers she had taken from her father's house. She wanted to examine the envelope from Elijah without Jesse being around. Although the envelope was empty, she thought maybe the missing contents could be found. As she reached for the envelope, Mirembee's heart stopped.

In the upper left-hand corner of a legal-size envelope, printed in bold letters, was "Farmers Mutual Life Insurance, Inc." Her hands shook as she examined the front and then the back of the sealed envelope. Willing her fingers to stop trembling and filled with anticipation, Mirembee carefully opened the envelope. Could it be? Did God really answer prayers? Inside, she found a standard policy paying ten thousand dollars, with double indemnity if the death was accidental, for a total of twenty thousand dollars. That was enough money to give CJ the kind of funeral Mirembee desperately wanted for her father. She could collect on the policy, pay Louise back, let Jesse keep his money, and if it was what CJ really wanted, she would let her unknown sisters and brothers share the rest. It was eight o'clock, and Mirembee thought to herself, they should be open.

Mirembee would have been satisfied with the two thousand dollars she needed for CJ's funeral, but an agent from Farmers

Mutual explained that the policy for Clarence James Williams had lapsed due to nonpayment. "The grace period expired nine days ago," the voice on the other end of the phone informed Mirembee.

The insurance adjuster apologized and said there was nothing he could do. He gave her the number for the home office, but the district manager didn't offer any more help. The insurance company's bureaucratic responses were full of rules and citations, leaving Mirembee frustrated.

Finally, yet unwilling to give up her fight for her father's dignity, she decided to take an action that was entirely out of character for the once-timid Mirembee.

By the time Jesse returned with thirteen hundred dollars, Amy gave him the extra three hundred. Mirembee was showered and dressed. Without informing Jesse, who was now sleeping, Mirembee took the money, stopped at the bank to cash Louise's check, and drove to the office of Attorney Richard M. Stock with thirty-three hundred dollars in cash in her purse.

Richard Stock was the only attorney Mirembee knew, so he would have to do, even though she only knew him by reputation. In Cleveland's black community, the Stock family had built a kind of empire. They owned a family grocery store, a funeral home, several beverage drive-thrus, a restaurant, a couple of police officers, and one politician, Congresswoman Elizabeth Stock-Burton, their sister.

Another brother managed the funeral home. That was the good side of the family.

On the other hand, not a single member of the Stock family had ever been convicted of breaking the law, thanks to Richard's expert lawyering. Rumor had it that Attorney Stock was the Malcolm X of the legal world: his unpublished motto was 'win by any means necessary.'

"I want you to sue Farmers Mutual Life Insurance Company," Mirembee told Attorney Stock.

"Sure," Stock said with a wry smile, "do you mind telling me exactly why I should sue them?"

Mirembee observed the man behind the cluttered desk. His attire matched the chaos of his office. The missing button that should have hidden his protruding stomach was absent, much like the inboxes that should have held the papers, now scattered randomly on and around his desk. Large gold and silver rings decorated the last two fingers on each of his chubby hands. Richard Stock was a stocky, stout man whose face looked like it was in the early stages of swallowing his eyes, nose, and mouth. It reminded Mirembee of a vacuum cleaner sucking in dirt as the bag filled up. But his eyes were sharp and quick as a calculator.

They owe me. My father paid that company for over ten years, and just because he missed the last payment by nine days—three of which he was dead—they refuse to pay. They say the grace period expired, and..." Attorney Stock shifted back, and the wooden, revolving pedestal chair creaked. "How much insurance are we talking about?" he asked, interrupting her mid-sentence. "Ten thousand dollars!" Mirembee quickly responded, and Stock calculated that meant three thousand and change in his pocket. Chump change. Of course, they would sue for more, but the company would probably settle for the face value. He could get his share without working too hard. "Do you have any paperwork? Correspondence, receipts?" "Will you take my case?" Mirembee demanded a commitment before showing him anything. She didn't have time to waste. "Well, I would like to see what you have before I decide." Attorney Stock was equally non-committal. "The policy doubles if the death was accidental," Mirembee watched his eyes calculate, and added, "That's seven thousand for you." She mentioned this ahead of Stock's calculations.

"I can tell you right now, it will be a tough case. The law is very specific. If you don't pay the premium, the policy is null and void. Maybe the insurance company will settle for half the face value, but I can't say for sure. A lawsuit can get pretty expensive. Are you the sole beneficiary?" Stock asked. Mirembee opened her purse and took out three thousand dollars.

Chapter 14

CJ Williams' Funeral

With the extra three hundred dollars Jesse gave her, Mirembee bought CJ a royal blue suit, a white shirt, and a red, white, and blue tie for his final public appearance. Lawrence Stock did not argue when she insisted that her father wear his new black shoes in the casket.

Even Louise and Lee attended the funeral, arriving late in the Lincoln to make an entrance, Mirembee thought. Louise paraded up the center aisle with Lee behind her, choosing to sit in the second row away from her daughter.

Jesse and Mirembee sat in the front row, holding hands. Most of the mourners were either people who worked with CJ or knew him from the bars. The leeches arrived, smelling of urine, beer, and unfiltered Camel cigarettes. A few curious strangers came to see this man in death, if not in life, about whom they had heard so much. The regulars, churchgoers who attended every funeral as a way to pass the time from their dull lives, sat in the back row near the aisle for a better view of the procession.

Typical, thought Mirembee of the mourners, all except Jesse's family; seven brothers, three sisters, ten shades of skin ranging from pale white to black, with their white mother and the strikingly beautiful woman and child sitting on the other side of the aisle. Flowers, without cards, since Lawrence Stock borrowed them from his other clients, perfumed the church. Mirembee wanted the funeral to be held at the biggest black church in the city, Mt. Olivet Missionary Baptist Church. A cousin of the Stock brothers was the church pastor, and they made it happen.

Choir members in royal blue robes with gold sashes sang as if Clarence James Williams were the prodigal son returning home to rest.

"Preeeecious Lord,

Take my hand,

Lead me oooooooon,

Let me stand."

Funeral regulars joined in, their voices blending with Mirembee and Jesse's quiet tears. A tall, bosomy, dark-skinned woman's powerful voice resonated through the church as she belted out, "Amazing Grace, how sweet the sound," leaving the entire congregation visibly moved. Rev. Dr. Emmanuel Stock garnered a chorus of "Amens" from the crowd as he spoke about God's plan for the homegoing of His children. Remarkably, he delivered the entire eulogy without mentioning CJ's name even once.

"Our brother has gone to a better place. Don't cry for him. He's in God's hands now. Cry for the sinners. Cry for yourselves if you have not called on Jesus. Call his name."

"Jesus!" the regulars cried out. "Jeeeeesus."

"Call on Him, uh, so you can meet your dearly departed walking up to the pearly gates, uh."

A chorus of "Jesus! Jesus! Jesus!" erupted from the regulars. A few stood, waving their hands in the air, and some of the leeches joined in with a sort of drunken dance.

"Call on Jesus if you want to meet your father in heaven, uh." The organist began playing the heavy bass chords in cadence with the minister's commands. "Call on the Rock of your salvation, uh. Call on the Son of God, uh. Call on Him."

In what seemed to be a spontaneous, simultaneous act, the organ and the minister first raised and then lowered the volume in their respective pipes. "Won't you just call on Him today? He wants you to give up your demons and join Him in the heavenly home He has prepared for you, just like He prepared for our dearly departed brother." Almost whispering now, Rev. Dr. Emmanuel Stock wiped the sweat from his forehead and concluded, "God has called his son home. One day, He will call you. Are you ready?"

Muffled whimpering replaced the loud cries throughout the sermon. The crowd had peaked and was now basking in the afterglow. Jesse was red eyed from all the tears shed for his dead father. Funeral regulars got what they came for, fuel for their conversation fire.

"That funeral was surely something to talk about," the regulars said.

"Rev. Stock sure knows he can preach."

"CJ was looking good."

"He still had all that hair from his Afro days."

"Must've dyed it, though. It was a lot darker than the last time I saw him."

"Somebody spent a whole lotta money on that man's homegoing."

"Could've been Louise. She looked like she got some money now."

"Or one of them other ladies CJ had."

"Yeah, he sure enough had some ladies." Their muffled laughter was not without notice.

Mirembee felt satisfied. It had been a good funeral. The Stock brothers hadn't let her down. Rev. Stock announced that the repast would be served in the social hall. Mirembee and Jesse waited to greet the mourners and spectators but didn't stay for the meal. That was for CJ's friends. A well-catered dinner, just as CJ would have wanted, was their final tribute to her father.

Mirembee cautiously introduced Jesse as her brother to those she knew, who had the decency to offer condolences before sitting down to eat. Their lack of surprise or suspicious looks confirmed her suspicion. They knew. The leeches knew. The fact that CJ had an outside child seemed more believable than unbelievable to most in attendance. If the others knew or suspected about Jesse, Louise must have known. Whether Louise knew or not was soon answered by her facial expression and demeanor when she saw Jesse. It was obvious that Jesse was half-white, although his skin was darker than expected, and he appeared to be younger than Mirembee. Even the beautiful lady with the child did not appear to question the sibling relationship between Mirembee and Jesse. Instead, she introduced herself as Kate, and the little girl as her daughter, Carmen.

Kate noticed the look on Mirembee's face when she mentioned Carmen's name. Mirembee stopped paying attention and focused on the little girl. She felt like she was looking at a younger version of herself. Carmen, one of the names in CJ's will.

While offering condolences, Kate slipped an envelope into Mirembee's hand, whispering for her to read it later. Mirembee placed the envelope in her purse, determined not to forget about it. She suspected it was money, judging by how wealthy this woman looked. Mirembee needed money, but neither the woman nor her envelope drew her attention. Instead, she kept studying the little girl.

Louise left the church, glad she hadn't given Mirembee the five thousand dollars and damning herself for giving her one single dime to put Clarence James Williams' white-cunt-eating ass in the ground.

Her abrupt exit from the church went unnoticed by the congregation, but a tall, handsome, dark-skinned man observed her departure from the back of the church. He had noticed her, and he wondered if she had paid for his father's funeral. He decided to ask his sister and brother.

Chapter 15
Kate

Colored lights flashed and trailed across the stage, highlighting the children for the cheering audience. Parents smiled proudly while their children, dressed in brightly colored costumes made of satin, peau de soie, and voile, tiptoed, twirled, and bounced through performance after performance during Miss Kate's School of Dance Annual Spring Recital.

The theatrical makeup designed to emphasize dramatic facial expressions for patrons sitting in the farthest rows seemed exaggerated from the closer seats, but it didn't distract from the youthful, lipsticked smiles and blue-shadowed eyes that paraded across the stage as Miss Kate's students made their final curtain call. Kate Johnson was not only the dance instructor, choreographer, director, and owner of the school; she was also the mother of the star performer.

Kate smiled warmly at CJ, who stood by the exit doors at the back of the theater. He watched their talented daughter, who bore a striking resemblance to her mother, with a mix of pride, admiration, and nostalgia.

It was the last time he would ever see mother and child in this life. His last child, he decided. He was old. He wasn't even sure how he managed to father this vibrant, full-of-life little girl.

Kate met CJ five years ago. He was fifty, and she was twenty-five, younger than Mirembee. Their chance meeting was just that—a chance meeting. Kate's dream of opening her own dance studio was about to come true. The only obstacle was getting the building wired correctly to meet the city zoning codes.

In an unusually bold move, Kate stood firmly outside the local electric workers' union hall, determined to find someone who could help her. Dressed in her bright red leotard, a white blouse that reached her waist, high heels, and a multi-colored scarf around her neck, Kate easily caught attention. Several men paused to look before going into the union hall.

"I need some help," she pleaded. Men stopped to listen but quickly shook their heads 'no' and walked into the hall, taking one last look at her breasts and butt. CJ liked her spunk as well as her creamy skin and auburn hair.

"What kind of help YOU need, young lady?" CJ said, evoking what was left of the old charm.

"Are you an electrician?" she asked, inspecting the shabbily dressed CJ with her eyes.

"If you need an electrician, then I am an electrician." CJ smiled.

"Let me see your license!" Kate demanded, instantly wishing she had been softer as she watched his full-length mirror eyes scan every curve and dip of her body. If CJ silently forgave the lack of respect in her voice, it was not obvious from his answer. "I'm like you, little lady, I don't need a license for what I do best."

Heat rose in her face as regret washed over her for not changing her clothes after teaching the last dance class. She wondered, what must I look like standing here trying to proposition men, even if it was for electrical work?

"Look," she said, much more subdued after this put-down. "I own a dance studio. "Well, I don't own it, I rent a studio. I want to create my own dance company. The city said I have to rewire the entire studio to meet code before I can open officially. The property owner will do it, but he wants to charge me two hundred more a month, and I just can't afford that. If I don't get the work done by the first..."

Despite all her bravado, Kate was starting to crack. CJ understood dreams and sensed that this young woman was trying to make a dream come true.

"Let's go have a cup of coffee. Maybe I can help you." CJ said.

CJ and Kate talked about their dreams for the next thirty days while CJ rewired the studio. He could have finished the whole job in two or three days, but working there gave him the chance to watch Kate dance. Some days, watching her made it hard to control the pounding in his chest and his pants.

When CJ announced that the project was finished and the studio had passed inspection, they celebrated with a bottle of Dom Perignon, saved for a special occasion, Kate said. Kate tried the red lights, then the blue lights. She turned on all the colored lights and the glass ball in the center of the room.

"C'mon, Mr. Clarence James Williams. Let's dance." Kate led the dance, but she did it so skillfully CJ felt he was being choreographed rather than directed. The music changed to a soft, mellow beat. Kate slipped herself under CJ's arms. Slowly, at first, CJ guided Kate through the bump and grind of old school, matching the dip of her hips with the rise of his. He held her so closely that her exhales became his inhales. Kate loved it. The feel of his strong body, even the faint fragrance of 3 in 1 oil and linseed extract in his clothes, heightened her awareness of his manhood. They kept dancing, even after the music stopped. Kate softly kissed him on the lips. "Thank you," she whispered.

The crystal ball above shimmered with tiny dots of light on the man and woman entwined below. CJ couldn't remember ever wanting a woman as badly as he wanted her. He kissed her passionately, making her gasp for breath at the force with which he held her. CJ couldn't bear it if she stopped him now; his once indefatigable ego had been bruised some time ago. CJ held her at arm's length and looked into her eyes. She returned the look as she began to take off her leotard. CJ stopped her by using his nimble fingers to gently roll the leotard down her shoulders, then planted a soft kiss on each exposed shoulder.

When her breasts were freed, CJ lowered her to the shining hardwood floor before removing the rest of her clothing. The phonograph clicked and another record dropped on the turntable. Billie Holliday sang of her man and CJ felt young again. He made love to Kate like a seasoned lover, timing his movements to extend the ecstasy until he was no longer in control. They heaved together after a simultaneous release.

The relationship lasted slightly over a year. Kate told CJ she was pregnant during a discussion about the rising student enrollment at the studio. CJ was surprised but relieved that Kate was handling the situation so well.

"I've always wanted a baby," she told CJ, "A little girl. I will teach her to dance and dance and dance." She said as she twirled around the room.

"What if it's a boy?" CJ asked, still amazed at her reaction to being pregnant by an old man.

"It won't be. I will have a girl. I'll name her Carmen after the French opera. Carmen de Milo, like Venus de Milo, the goddess of love."

"Carmen, who?" CJ wondered if Kate was losing her mind.

Carmen de Milo will be her stage name. Oh, CJ, she will be so famous. Won't it be wonderful?" Kate beamed. CJ didn't know what to say or do. The other women wanted him to marry them. That's it. She wants to get married, CJ thought. And why shouldn't he? It had been a long, long time since he busted up with Louise. If this beautiful young flower wanted to spend her youth blossoming in the arms of an older man, why not? At that moment, CJ realized that he was in love with Kate.

"Do you want to get married?" CJ asked. Kate stopped dancing in the middle of a turn, looked toward CJ, and laughed. It was as if she had taken a dagger and stabbed him in the heart. CJ stared at her in disbelief. Was she laughing at him? Kate immediately recognized the effect of her laughter and went from cold to hot in a second. She walked over to where CJ was seated and dropped to her knees in front of him.

"CJ, I have something to tell you." Her voice was low and plaintive. "I... I love you. Please always believe that I loved... love you. But..." her voice grew soft, "you are not the only one." CJ looked his flower child in the eyes. His eyes asked the questions that his mouth couldn't form.

"No, CJ, I don't just sleep around. There is a man. The one who helped me get this studio in the first place." CJ couldn't look at her. "I'm not even thirty years old. How do you think I got the money for all this?" she asked, waving her hand around the studio. CJ didn't answer. She stood up and continued, "He's married, and there's no chance he'll ever leave his wife and kids. But I know he will take care of... his baby and me. He's... rich."

Now CJ stood up. "His baby? How you know it's his?"

"It has to be CJ. Don't you see? He can give her everything. She will have the best schools, voice lessons, summer dance camps, and all the things those little rich girls have. She has to be his. You understand, don't you, CJ?" A look into Kate's brown eyes, and he understood. Kate was taking the path that led to easy street. It didn't take a genius to figure out that CJ had nothing. What Kate had with CJ was as good as it was going to get, but she yearned for more. More for herself and more for her child.

"Yes," CJ said. He understood that in this world, money makes a difference—not dignity, respect, or love. Money makes the difference.

The next time CJ saw Carman, she was scooting around the dance floor while her mother was instructing a group of preteens. He moved to the corner and picked up the baby. Carmen had the same gray/green eyes, mirroring all of CJ's children. CJ looked from child to mother, noticing similarities and differences.

"Okay, girls and boy," a reference to the only boy in ballet class which always brought smiles to the students, "You can get dressed now. See you next week. PRACTICE!" Kate called to the children, running to the dressing room, pausing only to kiss Carmen or say something to her before they left the studio.

Kate gave CJ a hard look before speaking. "Carmen's father is buying us a new studio uptown. He says that Carmen should have the best."

"She needs to know, Kate. It ain't right. She needs to know." CJ left the room, but more of him lingered in the air. Not yet, not now, Kate thought.

Over the years, CJ grew older, watching his daughter from afar. He wanted to tell Mirembee, but he didn't. He was surprised when he received a call from Kate. Carmen's benefactor father had passed away and left Carmen a substantial trust. She would never have to worry about money. Kate said it was time for Carmen to meet her father.

Carmen was a beautiful child, her mother deeply imprinted on her. Her beauty was rivaled by her talent. Carmen was scheduled to meet her real father the day after the fire. Another dream left unfulfilled disappeared in that fire.

Chapter 16

Elijah

By mutual agreement, Jesse moved in with Mirembee the day after the funeral. Their two modest, minimum-wage incomes would reduce Mirembee's reliance on Louise. Living together, they could make up for lost time and truly get to know each other. Additionally, CJ promised Jesse that they would one day live together, and Mirembee, sensing what it meant to Jesse, agreed.

"Are we going to try and find the others?" Jesse asked. "What if they're all like that, Elijah?" he continued. "I don't like him."

"I don't know." Mirembee replied, her mind drifting back to the scene at the church when the handsome, brown-skinned man approached her and Jesse, demanding, 'Who paid for this funeral?'

Both Mirembee and Jesse were taken aback. Mirembee recovered quicker and asked, "Who are you?"

"I asked you first, Honey. Who laid out this kind of money for the likes of him?"

Mirembee slapped him with all her might and fury. The regulars would have much to talk about tonight. "That's my father you're talking about," she screamed. The force of her slap caused his sunglasses to fly off his face. With slow, deliberate movements, he bent over to retrieve the glasses, but he didn't put them back on. Instead, he looked first at Mirembee, then at Jesse, and back to Mirembee. There was no mistaking his eyes.

"Well, I'm glad he was somebody's father."

"Eli, let's go." The small woman who had been with Elijah to the funeral tugged on his jacket sleeve. "Let's go, baby, c'mon." Without saying another word, Elijah and the woman walked out the door.

"Our brother?" Jesse queried.

"Yes," Mirembee said.

Chapter 17
Ohio Gas Company

While Jesse slept, something he did way too much of for Mirembee, she decided to sort and organize CJ's papers. She and Jesse had returned to the house after the funeral and found a few more letters and envelopes. Mirembee hoped they would reveal more information about their father's other life and their brothers and sisters.

When she saw the letter, she recalled that she had written to her father right before the abortion. She sobbed, recalling old memories of what might have been. Not wanting to prolong the misery, Mirembee placed the letter in a file marked "personal." The will was next, and she decided to make copies of it just in case, but in the meantime, she labeled a file "Daddy's Estate" and placed the will inside. An assortment of bills was put into a file marked "thirty days." She was surprised to find a bill from Higbees, especially when she noticed it was from the children's department. The purchase was made the day before CJ's death. It also went into the thirty-day file. She... Jesse's sleep sounds echoed in her mind... she and Jesse would ensure all of CJ's bills were paid. It's what Daddy would have wanted.

She noticed the unopened letter from the Ohio Gas Company. Mirembee opened it and read it. Ironically, it was dated the day CJ died.

January 26, 2001

Dear Mr. Williams:

Enclosed is a check in the amount of three hundred dollars, forty-three and fifty-seven cents ($343.57), which must be cashed within the next sixty days. Our records indicate that your check #32453, dated October 1, 2000, in the amount of three hundred forty-three and fifty-seven cents ($343.57) was incorrectly credited to the account of another customer.

We apologize for any inconvenience this delay may have caused you.

Sincerely,

Deborah A. Foxx

Customer Relations

"Jesse! Wake up!" Mirembee ran over to the bed to waken a startled Jesse. "Jesse, read this." She thrust the letter in front of his face. It was a much more difficult process for Jesse to wake up than for him to go to sleep. Gaining the necessary strength, he focused his eyes and read the letter.

"That's great, Rembee. We can definitely use the money to help pay your mother back for the funeral." Three hundred dollars wasn't much, and Jesse didn't understand why Mirembee had to wake him just to show him this letter.

"Jesse, don't you see? They are responsible! They're responsible for Daddy's death." Judging by the puzzled look on Jesse's face, Mirembee explained, "The gas was turned off, and that's why he had the heater. If the gas had been on, Daddy wouldn't have needed that heater. I remember now that Daddy told me he wasn't going to pay them again because he had already sent them a check. I was going to get the money from Louise and pay it for him, but he said no. It was the gas company's fault, and he had the canceled check to prove he had already paid.

Jesse understood. "Those cocksuckers!" was his initial response. "Too bad we can't sue their asses."

"Maybe we can," Mirembee said, her mind calculating. "Go back to sleep, Jesse. We'll figure it out tomorrow." Jesse easily complied with this request.

Mirembee looked at the stack of papers and wondered if there would be more surprises. Quickly, she skimmed the rest of the stack. She placed the gas company letter and the envelope with 'Elijah' in a small pouch at the back of her purse. That's when she noticed the envelope from the beautiful woman who came to the funeral. She pulled it from her purse, noticing for the first time that it was not just any envelope. The ecru-colored envelope was embossed with a two-line address on the back flap and sealed with a gold sticker. Inside was a handwritten note in a style so elegant it resembled calligraphy.

The note read: ***Rembee, call me, we need to talk.*** Enclosed was a business card for Kate's School of Dance. She placed the card next to the letter and the envelope in the back of her purse. She knew these issues required immediate attention. The Ohio Gas letter and the large envelope from the patent office were kept together in a separate file labeled Attorney Stock.

She had almost finished examining the papers when she noticed another sealed letter. She wondered, didn't Daddy ever open his mail? This one was from Consolidated Electronics, where CJ worked when Louise had him arrested, Mirembee recalled. She opened the letter. It was also dated a few days after CJ's death.

Dear Mr. Williams:

As a former employee of., you are entitled to receive funds owed you. When you terminated your employment, you did not receive your severance pay or bonuses earned through our employee suggestion plan.

Due to accumulated interest on both sums, the total amount accrued may be considerable. To settle this account in a timely manner, we request an immediate reply to this letter.

Please inform my office of your intentions by February 9. You may contact my office at 555-301-4707.

Sincerely,

Wilson Myers

President and CEO

General Electronic Inc

Mirembee looked at the clock. It was seven forty-five A. M. Chances are the offices were not opened yet, but she decided to try it anyway. To her surprise, the telephone answered on the first ring.

"Wilson Myers here." the voice said, startling Mirembee. Did the President and CEO of Consolidated Electronics answer his own phone before eight in the morning?

A bit perplexed, Mirembee said, "Mr. Wilson, my name is Mirembee Williams. My father, Clarence Williams, worked for your company. . . "

"Yes, yes," Wilson Myers interrupted as though waiting for this call, "Can I speak to your father, please?"

"My father is . . . my father died three days ago."

"I see. I mean, I'm genuinely sorry to hear that. You have my condolences. You are his daughter, you say?" Without waiting for an answer, he continued, "You must be calling about the letter."

Mirembee was starting to feel the heat from the fire in her stomach that refused to go out. Consolidated Electronics was a huge company, a multinational corporation. It was worth millions, probably billions. This man, Wilson Myers, must earn seven figures as the CEO. Yet here he was on the phone talking to little ole nobody, Mirembee Williams, probably using a private number since she did not go through a switchboard or a secretary. Smoke was beginning to rise from the heat...

"Yes, I found a letter among my father's possessions." Mirembee decided to proceed carefully.

"As you note in the letter, your father left our employment without settling some of his accounts. We would like to... to close the chapter on this one." The corporate jargon did not sit well with Mirembee. "Can we meet somewhere today or at your earliest convenience to discuss this?"

He's too eager, Mirembee thought. The fire in her gut blazed red hot. "Are you located in the city?" she asked.

"Our corporate headquarters are located on Superior Avenue."

"Where is your office?"

He did not expect these questions, so he answered quickly and honestly. "I'm on the twenty-second floor." The..." he paused, "executive suite."

"We can meet today," Mirembee announced. "I will come to your office. Goodbye." She hung up before a specific appointment time was scheduled. This was intentional; she didn't want Wilson S. Myers to be too prepared.

Within the next thirty minutes, Mirembee called off work for the day, showered and dressed in the smartly tailored black suit she wore to the funeral. Fifty-five minutes after she hung up the phone, she was seated on the twenty-second floor outside the corporate offices of Mr. Wilson S. Myers, President and Chief Executive Officer of Consolidated Electronics. She was grateful for her father's car.

"Come in, please, Ms. Williams." Mr. Myers' friendly manner was so exaggerated it came across as pretentious. It was clear that the security guards and secretaries had been warned to expect her arrival. She was quickly greeted at the main gate and led to the private elevator, which only stopped on the twenty-second floor. No one asked her for identification. Very strange.

The office was more luxurious than anything Mirembee had ever seen. Carpet, draperies, chairs, and wallpaper all matched in fabric and paint. There was no off-the-rack decorating here. Mirembee wasn't exactly sure what mahogany looked like, but she guessed that the wood that went a quarter of the way up the wall was mahogany. The desk, like the large oval table to the right of the door, had to be mahogany as well. Together, they were magnificent, highly polished works of art. Although her limited knowledge couldn't confirm it, Mirembee's eyes told her the paintings adorning the walls were originals. Mr. Myers offered her a chair and picked up the folder from his desk, which appeared very neat and organized—the polar opposite of Richard Stock's.

While Stock had to dig through mounds of scattered papers on his desk to find a pen, Mirembee couldn't help but notice that Myers had two Mont Blanc pen cases carefully aligned on the right side of his desk. The store where she once worked during the holiday season sold these pens for no less than $500 each. On the high end, Mont Blanc offered pens ranging from $1000 to $10,000 each (for an ink pen). Mirembee thought of this every time she passed the locked glass cases.

Myers, bred to dispense with social customs quickly, opened the folder and started explaining CJ's employment history with Consolidated Electronics. He briefly mentioned the employee suggestion plan. In his solitary speech, Myers noted that he had just become CEO six months ago and was working to resolve some lingering issues he inherited from the previous CEO. Mirembee listened without saying a word. Myers continued, "So we owe your father, I mean you, thirty thousand dollars," he said, smiling at Mirembee. "I have the check right here. All you need to do is sign a few papers and it's yours." Still smiling, he handed the check to Mirembee.

Mirembee stood up and let her eyes scan the wealth in this room once more. The tapestry carpet beneath her feet made her want to take her shoes off. Louise and Lee had money, but this... this was obscene wealth. Returning her gaze, CJ's gaze, to the CEO, presumably the highest-paid person in this company, she spat out, "Screw you!"

In her mind, thirty thousand dollars wouldn't pay for the glass-engraved coasters on the table. How can thirty thousand be enough to pay for her father's mind? He was owed much more, and she wasn't going to let this bloated, egoistic, fat man cheat him out of it.

Mirembee turned and hurried through the double doors of the executive suite, leaving Wilson S. Myers standing in the middle of the office with his mouth and fly open.

Returning home, Mirembee found Jesse still sleeping. She removed her clothing, slipped on a housecoat, and got into the bed next to her brother. She closed her eyes, but sleep eluded her. Thoughts and questions swirled in her mind. First, her baby, and now her father— the only two people she loved were gone. Why, God? Why are the ones I love taken away from me? Jesse's snoring interrupted her thoughts. Why had CJ told Jesse about me and not tell me about Jesse?

Thinking about her father, she quietly asked, "Is a man judged by the way he lived his life or the way he ended it?" Mirembee cried. Jesse stirred.

Book Two

Throughout her young life, she has tried to please her father, never quite realizing that, as a girl, she never could.

— Alice Walker

Chapter 18

Victoria

The first time Victoria had sex, she got pregnant. She couldn't understand it. She was not one of those trailer trash girls who let every boy walk all over her. She was a Yale law student with top grades in her class. Sure, she knew some Yale coeds who were doing it, with and without protection. But Yale girls were not like those other girls. Twenty-three-year-old law students with a BA in Political Science and taking graduate courses at Yale Law didn't get pregnant.

Why me? She thought. How will I ever be able to explain this to my parents? Her parents were enlightened, but. . . a baby out of wedlock was definitely not in their plans for Victoria.

Six years ago, Victoria, then seventeen, successfully completed honors courses and was ready to graduate from Phillips Academy Andover. It had been a great year, although she initially resisted the idea of attending a private preparatory school for her secondary education, especially a boarding school, but her parents insisted, and she relented. She decided it was a good decision as she delivered her final speech as the president of her graduating class.

Teachers and students alike were in awe of Victoria. While the combination of beauty and intelligence was common at school,

Victoria embodied both qualities, earning her unanimous selection as Homecoming Queen and Most Likely to Succeed. Keys to a new car were traditional gifts for Andover graduates, but a sleek new black 380 SL Mercedes-Benz two-seater convertible was a bit showy even for an Andover graduate.

Completing her studies at Andover in three years and graduating Summa Cum Laude made the transition to Yale Law School easy. Her grades, LSAT score, and her parents' monetary donation made her a shoo-in.

Victoria Lynn McMillen was the adopted daughter of J. Clyde and Lynda Kay Burness McMillen. After losing their first and only biological daughter when she was six months old, the McMillens tried unsuccessfully to conceive again. As Lynda Kay approached her fortieth birthday, the thought that she might never become a mother again almost overwhelmed her. J. Clyde loved his wife more than anything else in the world, which is how he justified his numerous affairs. He did not love any of the others. Watching his wife sink deeper into depression was more than J. Clyde could handle. She had stopped eating, sleeping, and bathing. Some weeks, she would stay in her pajamas all day. When she hadn't gotten out of **bed** for an entire week, J. Clyde knew he had to do something. When you are rich and money is no object, you do what you must to help. J. Clyde would save his wife's life by buying her a baby if necessary.

He immediately regretted the decision to see this child before the adoption was finalized. He failed to ignore the unexplained feelings he was experiencing about the child he planned to give his wife. Once Lynda Kay saw, held, and kissed the baby, the obsession started. He never wanted to see the look he knew would return to Lynda's eyes if she lost this child, too. J. Clyde prayed that the child he went to great lengths and paid $50,000 for would help Lynda recover from the darkness that had taken over her since the death of their beloved child. J Clyde lived long enough to never regret, not even for a moment, the money spent to buy this child for his wife. Lynda Kay not only accepted this new baby but also cherished her, giving her the same name she had given their firstborn, Victoria Lynn.

The following years found Lynda so absorbed in every aspect of Victoria's life that J. Clyde feared that Lynda Kay had replaced depression with obsession. In her first year, the child took over his wife, leaving little room for his wishes and wants. Fears that his wife had lost control were eased as Lynda Kay combined love with the right amount of discipline.

They had argued over the adoption of a mixed-race child, but Lynda Kay's tears, pleadings, and threats won.

She's a baby. A baby, J. What do we need to know? It doesn't matter to me what her parents' race is. Many people adopt Asian, South American, or even Russian babies. I want her. I love her.

"But she is not Asian or South American. The lawyer said, "Her mother is white and her father is black."

"I don't care! Damn it, J! She needs us. You saw her face, her eyes, those beautiful eyes. J. please."

"But darling, I'm sure if we wait, we will be able to find a baby we want."

"No, J. I can't wait!" J. Clyde knew this was spoken truth. His wife could not wait. It was now or never. So, he greased the palms that needed greased, and kissed the asses that needed kissed until Lynda Kay got her baby. J. Clyde and Lynda Kay McMillen left the offices of Cline, Horowitz & Stein, LLC with the six-day-old baby girl in their arms.

Victoria was told about her adoption and her mixed parentage as soon as she could understand the concept, which, for a precocious child, meant she was every bit of four years old. The news did not negatively affect her, even as her understanding grew. She loved her parents and was very grateful for the lifestyle they had given her. Besides, she had Lynda Kay's dark hair and J. Clyde's good looks, but most importantly, she looked white. If the topic of her adoption didn't come up, she didn't bring it up.

The fact that she was accepted into the most prestigious law schools, including Stanford, Harvard, Yale, and Duke, did not surprise anyone. Victoria chose Yale. She often referred to law school as 'easy,' a comment that did not sit well with her fellow classmates. Victoria was sailing along, focused and directed when she met Will.

Willford A. Headley, Jr. was almost handsome. It wasn't his physical appearance that caught Victoria's and the other first-year female law students' attention. Will had an intangible quality, a certain 'IT' factor, a sexual aura that infused every aspect of his presence. His slow walk. His swag. His smile, which started with a slight upturn of his full lips and ended with a flash of his professionally straightened white teeth. It was as if he planned it. He never quite turned it off, but he saved its most powerful effect for when he needed it. He needed it now if he was going to get through law school.

Will's admission to law school was due to affirmative action. His father, Willford Headley, Sr., had deep pockets and used his wealth and influence to ensure that university officials would act favorably regarding his son's application. Sadly, his father's money could not guarantee Will's academic success.

Will knew he could not fail. His father was understanding but demanding. Will could not be the one Headley son who would not reach the top of his profession. His father worked very hard to make Headley a household name in American politics, and he needed his sons to climb the ladder he laid out for them. Visions of dynasty danced in his mind. At the very least, he expected one of his sons to become president of the United States, probably Will. He had the look. Although he was not very bright, he was clever enough. A Yale law degree would certainly give him an advantage.

During the first quarter, Will found himself between a rock and a hard place. Should he tell his father he was failing law school or wait until the university officials sent quarterly grades home? Either way, he was up the creek without a paddle unless... the thought came to him during his Civil Procedures class.

Professor Thantakaisis called on the class to review the court findings in Fuller v Illinois. One student, the attractive girl with the strange eyes and a full head of curly black hair, volunteered to review the case, reciting the case history, describing the litigants, highlighting the court findings, and beginning to list the issues that allowed the defendants to appeal to the district court when Professor Thantakaisis said, "Thank you, Victoria."

After class, Will followed Victoria out of the lecture hall. "Hey," he called. "Wait a minute." When he caught up with her, he said, "That was pretty impressive. How did you know all of that? I mean, how do you remember all of those facts?"

"It's eas. . . ," she caught herself before finishing, knowing how most of her classmates reacted when she said law school was easy. "I work very hard studying," she smiled.

"My name is Will Headley," he said, turning on the twenty-four-carat smile. "And you are Victoria...?"

"McMillen."

"Well, Victoria McMillen, would you like to go for a soda or something?"

Victoria's first instinct was to decline, but there was something about this young man with the shining smile. She hesitated and then said, "Thirty minutes, and then I must study. Okay?"

"Sure," Will replied, "I need to do some studying myself." They spent the next six hours together, discussing, studying torts and business law. The following day, Will volunteered to review the facts involving Sheldon v IBX, Inc.

Will and Victoria became a common sight on the quad, in the library, and in lecture halls across campus. He, the youngest of three Headley brothers—all Yale graduates and corporate executives—benefited from a powerful father with political and economic ties reaching all the way to the White House. She was beautiful, wealthy, and smart with a pedigree family background.

They shared classes, and Will persuaded Victoria to switch her focus to political law, a move she willingly made, knowing she had already completed most of the courses needed for her desired corporate law concentration. Under Victoria's guidance, Will's grades improved significantly. The senior Headley was immensely proud of his son.

Will should have realized, but he didn't. Victoria was falling in love with him. Although she never voiced or acted on her feelings, she looked forward to their time together. She had long sensed what Will wanted from her, and she didn't mind being around him. As they neared the end of their third year, Victoria feared it might be the end of their relationship. Her fears eased somewhat when Will suggested they spend the six weeks between graduation and the bar exam studying together. Victoria was thrilled.

Will's father paid for a duplex in New Haven after graduation. In hindsight, Victoria wished she had enrolled in the dual degree program as she initially planned before meeting Will. Since she hadn't, she focused on earning an MBA while studying for the bar. When she wasn't in class, she was with Will. All that closeness led to the inevitable—one night, one moment, one unprotected act of giving and receiving, and Victoria was pregnant.

Will accepted the news with a mixture of pain and hopelessness. He liked Victoria well enough, but he simply didn't know what to do. Not being one to make important decisions without his father's guidance, Will found comfort in a bottle of Jack Daniels. Armed with a good deal of liquid courage, he summoned the strength to call his father.

"What's her name?" the senior Headley asked.

"Victoria. . . Victoria McMillen. You've met her." Will offered.

"Her parents' names?" This question was his father's only response.

"Her father is J. Clyde McMillen and her mother's name is Lynda," Will answered hesitantly. "Dad, do you think. . . "

The senior Headley interrupted. "I'll get back to you."

Wilford Headley, Sr. hung up the phone and immediately picked it up again. When his party answered, he spoke softly into the phone, "It's me. I have a job for you."

By five o'clock that evening, Wilford Headley, Sr. was on the phone with his son.

"You are going to marry that girl." He announced.

"But, Dad, I don't know if she wants to marry me. I don't even know if she even wants to have the baby."

"Is it your baby?"

"Yes!"

"You're sure."

"Yes. Yes. Dad, it was only one time. We were studying…"

Now listen to me, Will. I had her and her family checked out. They are a good family. Connected. You could do a lot worse than marrying into the McMillen family. Your mother will call her mother and make all the arrangements. You can get married right after you both pass the bar.

Will had not anticipated his father's reaction. He was a good son and if this is what his father wanted, then so be it. "I'll tell…"

"Ask!" his father boomed.

"I'll ask Victoria tonight. Thank you, Dad."

Victoria was deliriously happy. Having enjoyed an open relationship with her parents, she was now eager to tell them about her pregnancy along with the wonderful news of her wedding. Her heightened emotions eased slightly when her mother asked, "Victoria, do you think you should tell him?"

"No, mother, not unless he asks," Victoria responded, feeling a bit deceptive. "I love him. I will make him the best wife he could ever possibly have."

Will was consumed with doubt. Was Victoria the one? For the rest of his life? He cared for her. She had helped him through law school. She was beautiful, and his father said she came from a good, connected family. He believed this union would benefit both Victoria and him. But, did he love her?

Wilford Headley, Sr. reread the report and threw it into the fireplace. He had no reason to doubt its accuracy because his sources were always thorough and trustworthy. However, this time, his investigators were careless. Since Victoria shared the same name as McMillen's first child, because the adoption didn't follow standard legal procedures, because the McMillens were a respected family, and because it was Friday, the investigator didn't think to investigate further. The initial report was sealed and sent by carrier to Wilford Headley, Sr.

The wedding of Victoria Lynn McMillen and Willford Ashford Headley, Jr. was the social event of the season for the country's business and political elite. Local hotels were filled with reservations from major cities on both the East and West Coasts. Headley claimed that the ambassadors to England and France flew back to the United States solely to attend his son's wedding, along with the California and Seattle elite.

There was an unusual atmosphere of cooperation between the two families. Both sets of parents were extremely pleased with their child's choice of partner. A series of parties started right after they took the bar exam. For Victoria, the whirlwind of activity was like a fairy tale come true. She loved every moment of it. Will pretended, for his parents' sake as well as Victoria's, to be completely happy. He played the doting fiancé as best he could, while he worried about passing the exam. Every conscious moment, he rehearsed ways to tell his father that he had failed the bar. He knew Victoria would pass and she had helped him prepare, but he doubted his own ability.

Victoria looked beautiful on her wedding day. The sun had given her a lovely tan, making her eyes stand out more against that golden skin. The bride and her attendants carried White Calla Lilies accented with greenery and sprinkled with Lilies of the Valley. Fragrance and floral arrangements filled the grounds of the Headley estate.

Victoria wore a floor-length gown of antique satin designed by a French designer recommended by her future mother-in-law.

The Headley men wore their gray tails, which were always reserved for the most special occasions. There was a telegram of regrets from President and Mrs. Reagan for not being able to attend, but Vice President Bush, Mrs. Barbara Bush, several senators, congress members, and a few cabinet members were present. It was a grand and glorious day that ended with the happy couple leaving for a month-long honeymoon cruising the Greek Isles. Victoria thought it was extravagant, but her new father-in-law convinced her that they should consider the cruise a combined gift for graduation, the wedding, and a celebration for passing the bar.

Passing the bar had Will, Jr. agitated. He was consumed by these thoughts throughout the wedding preparations and honeymoon.

Will was so absorbed in thoughts of himself and his future that he barely noticed his future wife. It wasn't until the honeymoon that he began to see Victoria differently. He had always respected her mind, and now he was starting to appreciate her body as well. Their one-time lovemaking before the wedding was nothing like this. Victoria was vibrant, sensual, and sexy. Will wondered how he had missed this side of her. Heads turned wherever they went. Greek men openly commented on her beauty. "Ti oraia ginaika," oh, what a beautiful woman, the men shouted as the newlyweds walked the cobbled streets. Will found himself falling deeply, profoundly in love with his wife. For a while, he forgot about the bar exam and gave his mind, body, and soul to Victoria.

When they returned from the honeymoon, the Headleys insisted that the couple take the house by the lake. "There is no sense worrying about starting work now. Besides," reasoned Willfred, Sr., when the bar results are announced in a few days, the job choices will be much better."

Victoria readily entered the nest-building stage. She and Will transformed the extra walk-in closet into a small nursery so the baby would be close by. She couldn't have been happier. Her collapse happened while she was painting the baby's room. The doctor explained it was a miscarriage, likely caused by food or water consumed while out of the country. The outlook for future children was positive, but Victoria needed to rest now. He recommended waiting six months to a year before trying to get pregnant again. Victoria and Will were devastated. Their shared loss strengthened their love. It was Wilfred, Sr., who delivered the news that lifted their spirits.

As Victoria lay in the hospital bed with Will holding her hand, Willfred, Sr. announced that the results were in and they had both passed the bar exam. Will, Jr. couldn't believe it. He had passed. Based on his son's reaction, Will, Sr. wondered if he should have told his son that an old law school buddy was grading the exam this year. A few telephone calls confirmed that his friend would grade Will's exam. He made no arrangements for Victoria's exam. If she failed the first time, that would prove Will, Jr.'s superiority over her, which Wilfred, Sr. believed was necessary for a good marriage.

Chapter 19

Attorney Stock

Attorney Robert Stock was on the transmitting end of the telephone when Mirembee answered.

"Hello."

"Am I speaking to Mir…Mir…embee Mirembee Williams?"

"Rembee Williams. Yes."

"This is Attorney Richard Stock. I have good news."

"Good news?"

"Yes! The insurance company wants to settle." The silence on the other end of the line prompted Stock to ask, "Are you there?" Actually, he was familiar with that kind of reaction from his clients. The silence was usually followed by one question, 'how much?' He waited for Mirembee to ask.

Instead, he heard, "We will be in your office within the hour."

Mirembee hung up the telephone as Stock was saying, "Aren't you going to ask me how much they offered?"

The obvious similarity between the two people seated in front of him was unmistakable. Their shared distinctive eyes immediately caught his attention. Mirembee introduced Jesse and then explained the will.

"This means that any award you receive must be shared among the six siblings, minus our fee, of course." Stock said.

"Of course," Mirembee said, understanding that money was the driving force behind Stock's actions.

I am assuming the will is valid and properly probated, or else other beneficiaries could claim a stake in the estate. On the other hand," Attorney Stock was offering them a way out of this perceived dilemma, "a handwritten will, not filed or probated, could be considered a fraud and thus open to a contested claim.

"The will is valid. This is," Mirembee looked at Jesse and continued, "our father's handwriting. This is what he wanted. We are to share the proceeds from his estate among the six siblings. I am the administrator," Mirembee said.

"So, you all agree?" Attorney Stock asked, then immediately followed up with another question. "Where are the others? Why aren't they here?"

Mirembee explained in detail about finding the will, meeting Jesse, the exchange with Eli at the church, and the fact that she had no idea who or where the others were. Stock's facial expression showed he was less than happy about this turn of events. Now what? A mess like this could be tied up in court for years. Shit! He will have to work for this money. Damn!

"How much?" Mirembee's voice cut into his thoughts.

"What?" Stock said.

"How much did they offer?"

"Face Value. Ten thousand dollars."

"Face Value," Mirembee said incredulously. "Why?"

"The company is battling some big-time lawsuits involving clients the EPA is going after. They don't want to tie up their legal team with chump change."

For the first time, Jesse spoke, "Ten thousand dollars! Chump change."

"The EPA wants millions, hundreds of millions," Stock said, turning to Jesse.

"How much would it cost us to hire somebody, you know, a private detective, to find our brothers and sisters?" Mirembee asked.

"That depends," began Stock, "A top-notch investigator . . ."

"How much!" Mirembee's voice was several octaves higher than it needed to be. Atty stock appeared perturbed.

"Between ten and fifty thousand, depending on the time and the amount of work."

"Tell the insurance company we are demanding an additional ten thousand for double indemnity. You'll still get the half I promised you and your brother?" Stock shook his head, thinking if he got the extra ten, he would also be entitled to half of that. "I want you to use the extra money to hire someone to find our sisters and brothers. When you find them, I will get them to agree to give the entire twenty thousand to you." Jesse turned to his sister, but the look on her face silenced his words. "Here," she handed Attorney Stock a copy of the will, the envelope with Elijah's name, and the business card from Kate's School of Dance. "This might help, Mr. Stock," she rose, followed by Jesse. "When you find my sisters and brothers, we are going to sue for millions, hundreds of millions," Mirembee stated.

Chapter 20

Franklin (Frank) Evans

Frank Evans had a small hustle going. The used car lot was turning a good profit, most of which the majority was reported to the IRS. He had a fox for a girlfriend and could get as many ladies on the side as he wanted.

Frank was careful to keep his business ninety percent legal. The last thing he needed was to get busted selling used cars with rolled-back odometers. If his customers were too naïve to ask, he didn't bother to tell them when a car had been repaired after a bad wreck or pulled from a flooded lake. He understood that a thorough check wouldn't be done on him; after all, both he and his customers shared the same racial background. Still, he was a little suspicious of the man in the suit who was walking toward his office. He looked like the heat.

"Could I have a moment of your time, Mr. Evans?" the man said.

"The salespeople will be glad to help you," Frank responded.

"I didn't come to buy a car."

Frank was nervous. He slid his hand under his desk and removed the gun mounted there. "Well, what did you come for?"

"I work for a client who has reason to believe that you might be related to her."

Still cautious, Frank said, "I ain't related to nobody, man."

"Mr. Evans, my client believed that her father, Mr. Clarence James Williams, was also your father. Mr. Williams died two months ago and there are questions involving the estate." Frank put the gun back in its mount. His interest was piqued now.

"I am not at liberty to say any more currently. Your sister requests that you meet with her and her attorney on Monday at 8:00 A. M. Here is the address." He handed Frank a card, rose and started for the door.

"Sister! Wait a minute," Frank called after him, "what's her name?"

"I'm sorry, but I have been instructed not to divulge that information." He stopped at the door, "Mr. Evans, it is in your best interest to attend this meeting."

Frank Evans was waiting in the living room of his mother's small, modest home when she came back. She had never stopped going to church, and she entered the house, surprised to see her son there.

"Frankie, it's good to see you. I wish you would come around more often."

"My father," Frank demanded. "Who is he?" The question startled Evelyn. She stopped in the middle of removing her coat and hat. She had never been able to outwit her son. Her mind told her, 'Tell him the truth, the whole truth.'

Frankie, I've tried to tell you about him before... I've always wanted to tell you all these years. But you never cared or acted like you wanted to know.

"Tell me now," Frank demanded. "I want to know now." Evelyn kept removing her church-going hat and sat in the chair facing her son. Slipping off her shoes, she studied Frank's face. What she saw there was resolve. Evelyn was unsure how to take her one and only offspring. She decided to share the entire long, painful story with her son.

When I was a small child, my daddy, your granddaddy, died while we was living in Ohio the first time. Momma and I moved back to Georgia to live with her mother, greatgram, on the farm. Greatgram started keeping company with a man named Mr. Perkins..." Frank remembered Mr. Perkins's name because everyone called him Poppa Perkins, although he did not ever remember seeing or meeting him. Frank thought Mr. Perkins was his grandfather. You mean Poppa wasn't my real grandfather?

Please, Frankie, let me jest tell you the whole story.

174

Everything was fine for a while. Then Mr. Perkins said he wanted to move north to Ohio. So Momma, me, Greatgram, and Mr. Perkins jest up and left the farm and came here. Momma didn't want to go back to Ohio, and neither did I. We had lost her husband and my father there. Most of our memories weren't happy or pleasant.

His mother's eyes filled with tears. "That's when it started, when we came back to Ohio." Momma got sick the first winter after we moved. They couldn't save her. She died in her sleep, and I was the first to wake up and find her." She paused while she dried her tears and blew her nose. Frank said nothing.

"Mr. Perkins came into my room the day after we buried Momma. Then he comes most every night. At first, he… jest touches me. Then he made me touch him and…."

"Poppa was my father?" Frank asked incredulously, not wanted his mother to reveal any more gruesome details.

"No! No! No! Twern't him. Your daddy saved me from him. He saved me from dem hoodlum boys that were always picking on me, too. I didn't want to tell him bout ole Mr. Perkins, but he kept axing me. Finally, I just told him. Yo daddy says to me, 'Don't you worry bout him no mo. I promise he ain't never gonna bother you no mo.' I don't know what he did, but Mr. Perkins went away and never did touch me again. Anyway, I was just so grateful I thanked him in the only way I knew how. All dose years wit old Mr. Perkins, and my seed never got caught. One night wit your daddy and I was knocked up." Frank couldn't believe it. His mother was smiling. "Your daddy is Clarence James Williams, a fine man."

Frank's voice broke the silence after his mother's admission. "I don't understand. If he was such a good man, why didn't he accept his responsibilities? Why have I gone all these years without a father? Why did you have to work so hard? And why did we have to live with Greatgram in the first place?"

"CJ, that's what everybody called him. He didn't know at first. He thought you were Mr. Perkins' child. I didn't tell him no difference because, see, I weren't the onliest one knocked by yo daddy. There were at least three of us, maybe more. At least, that was the talk. One of them girls was 'posed to be white and real rich. The other one, Lucy, was CJ's girlfriend, and everybody was afraid of her 'cause she was so wild and mean. She would fight a man twice her size. Least for that, stuff took over her. I don't know anything about the others. Back then, they didn't let pregnant girls go to school, so Greatgram made me stay in the house for almost a year. I never did go back to school. I had to take care of you and Greatgram.

"Did you see him again?" Frank asked.

"Yes, and when he saw you, I didn't hafta tell him you were his child. He knew. He never did say nothin, but he knew. He started sending us little things. I had to tell him to stop. He was married by that time and struggling himself. I told him we were all right. He told me it was up to me to tell you. I tried, but you didn't seem like you cared, and well, I just didn't feel like anything good would happen by bringin it up again after all dese years."

Frank, focusing on his mother's face, said, "Well, you don't have to worry about it any longer. Clarence James Williams is dead." Frank marveled as he watched his mother's face crumble. Always thin and slight, Evelyn Evans seemed to be vanishing inward, shedding tears silently, her face showing a weariness far beyond her years.

"CJ was a good man, Frankie," Evelyn said when she was able to compose herself, "A good man."

Chapter 21

Kate and Carmen

Mirembee made a personal call to Kate and Carmen. She was surprised to find a moving van and movers packing Kate's place. Kate immediately recognized Mirembee. "Come on in, honey," she said. "Forgive the mess, but we're moving to California."

"California?"

"Yes, Carmen auditioned for a part on Yesterday, Today and Tomorrow and she got it." Kate was flying.

Mirembee felt it was her duty to bring her back down to earth. "Was CJ your father?"

"CJ?" Kate looked puzzled.

"Clarence James Williams."

Kate stopped and looked at Mirembee, then she laughed. "No, Rembee, he was Carmen's, my daughter's, father." That's right, thought Mirembee, the name on the will was Carmen, not Kate. The fact that Kate called her Rembee did not escape Mirembee's notice. Only CJ and now Jesse called her Rembee.

Mirembee stared at the beautiful woman who appeared to be younger than she and Jesse.

Kate proceeded to explain the agreement she and CJ had. Since she trusted Mirembee, she even confided in her about the trust Carmen's 'father' left her. With the trust and Carmen's new gig on the TV show, Kate figured that she and Carmen were set for life. Kate was not interested in pursuing a lawsuit against anybody.

"We need your signature. Mirembee stated, "Since Carmen is a minor, we need her to waive her share of the estate or join us in the suit."

Look, Rembee, Carmen has enough money. I expect this soap is just the beginning. Carmen is an extremely talented girl. I'll sign the waiver if it helps you. But I do not want my daughter's name involved in any legal business.

"Thank you very much," Mirembee said genuinely grateful. "One more thing before I go. Can I meet Carmen?"

"Of course," Kate agreed, "But remember, she doesn't know. I will tell her when I know the time is right."

"Okay."

The meeting with Carmen went exceptionally well. Mirembee regretted not bringing Jesse along. As Kate had predicted about her daughter, Carmen was an extraordinarily talented child. Hollywood was ready to embrace this young talent with open wallets.

Chapter 22
Attorney Stock

"I'm sorry, Ms. Williams; our investigators are unable to find anyone named Jill who might be related to you. Elijah was easy..." Attorney Stock paused, considering whether revealing how simple it was to locate Elijah might somehow decrease his share of the lawsuit proceeds. "It was easy to convince Elijah that he needed to be at the meeting once we shared the details and the possibility that there was some money in it for him," Stock said.

"How did you locate Elijah?"

"Your brother has an extensive...um public record. It appears he has spent considerable time living in Ohio Correctional Institutions. Atty Stock was unsure of how Mirembee would react. He found her very unpredictable.

"I see," said Mirembee. "Schedule the meeting anyway, a week from today. Your office, just as we planned?"

"Yes, of course. That's fine. Uh, Mr. Frank Evans will be here Monday at 8:00 AM."

"I've decided not to meet with him without the others. I want you to keep the appointment. Explain everything to him. Feel him out. If he's not willing to come to the meeting, then I will talk to him."

"Okay. Should I tell him everything?"

"Yes. And one more thing. I don't want to meet him, but I do want to see him. Is there a place where..."

Richard Stock appeared to read her mind. "Yes, the conference room has a two-way mirror."

Mirembee was not surprised by this revelation. She rose to leave. "I have Kate's promise," she said, putting on her coat. "She is willing to sign a waiver for Carmen. What can we do about Jill?"

"We may be able to file in absentia for her. I'll research it."

"Good. See you Monday."

Jesse and Mirembee arrived at the meeting at 7:00 AM. Based on Mirembee's assessment of Frank after observing him through the two-way mirror, she expected him to come early. Frank arrived at 7:30 and was kept waiting in the reception area. Elijah was late, arriving around 8:45. At nine o'clock, four of CJ Williams' children were seated at a large conference table in the offices of Attorney Richard Stock.

Mirembee introduced herself. Jesse listened, Frank scowled, and Elijah said, "What the fuck are we doing here?"

"We're here because our father left a will," Mirembee began.

She was interrupted by Stock, who said, "Ms. Williams, perhaps I can best relate the events which bring us together at this moment." Mirembee acquiesced with a nod of her head. Her brothers were new to her, and she took the opportunity to evaluate them.

Attorney Stock began by recalling his first visit with Mirembee. He explained how he accepted much less than his normal fee because he wanted to help them. He elaborated on his efforts to persuade his brother, Lawrence Stock, to provide a wonderful funeral for CJ. Elijah glared at Mirembee. Mirembee and Jesse returned the stare.

Stock carefully relayed the next series of events without revealing the insurance company's latest offer. "Mirembee," he said, asked that he attempt to locate the other children. Everyone has been located but Jill. There is no trace of her. We only had a first name, he said in defense of his efforts. The other girl is quite young, but her mother is willing to represent her interests. Both Frank and Elijah said, "How young is she?'

"She's ten." This was the first time Mirembee had spoken since Stock interrupted her. It was clear to everyone in the room that Mirembee was retaking charge. "The company is offering to pay the insurance policy at face value. Ten thousand dollars, but we are asking for double indemnity for accidental death. That means we want the full twenty thousand." she announced. She had gotten her brothers' attention.

"That's twenty thousand divided six ways minus his cut." Frank sneered at Stock. Elijah sat straight up, calculating his share.

"No!" Mirembee was less than kind. "Before you start spending our father's insurance…" Both men were on their feet.

"Father!" Frank shouted, "I ain't had no damn fa. . ." He stopped, thinking he was about to talk himself out of a sizeable chunk of change.

"When do I get my share of our father's money?" Elijah made *father* sound like a cuss word.

Jesse, who had been quiet up to this point, shouted, "Sit down! Rembee oversees our father's estate." he emphasized the last two words. There is more. Listen to what she has to say."

The brothers sat down, and Mirembee continued. "I think it's time I talk to my brothers alone." Stock obediently left the room. Mirembee suspected he had other means of monitoring the conversation, including the two-way mirror Mirembee used to watch Frank. "There is more," she repeated. The two brothers listened as Mirembee explained how CJ died. The brothers remained unemotional.

Copies of the gas company letter were handed to Frank and Elijah. Without responding to their puzzled looks, Mirembee then gave them copies of the letter from Consolidated Electronics. After they finished reading both letters, Mirembee said, "The gas company is responsible for CJ's death." She deliberately chose not to use the term father, and Consolidated owes him, uh, us for his work. We are going to sue both."

"Millions," Jesse said, "hundreds of millions!"

Chapter 23

Evelyn Evans

Regular meetings for Mirembee, Jesse, Frank, and Elijah were considered necessary over the next several weeks. They gathered in Stock's office whenever their attorney's involvement was needed, and Kate was conference-called in by phone. Otherwise, the siblings met at Mirembee's and Jesse's little apartment. Frank listened to stories about CJ. Even Elijah talked about the year he lived with CJ. Jesse expressed surprise that CJ never mentioned Elijah or Frank to him. Mirembee said she was surprised to learn about each of her siblings.

The conversation about father bonding made Frank think of Paula. Frank almost forgot about her, just as he thought his father had forgotten about him. Since Frank had no stories about CJ, he shared tales from his childhood scams.

Mirembee told them about Kate and Carmen, highlighting how beautiful and talented Carmen was. They agreed it would be incredibly exciting to see someone related to them on television every day. Elijah fell noticeably silent when the topic shifted to their mothers. Their conversations revealed that the brothers cared more for their mothers than Mirembee did for hers. Once, Jesse, who usually didn't say much, told them about Amy and his other brothers and sisters. Elijah, who thought Jesse was weak and a flunky to

Mirembee, made a crude remark about white women being on welfare and having more children with black men than black women did.

Frank stopped what was about to become a physical confrontation between Elijah and Jesse. "Wait a minute," Frank said to Jesse, "Is your mother white?" The three of them looked at Frank as if to question his intelligence. To the others, Jesse's parentage was obvious.

"Yes," Jesse answered while trying to muster enough anger to lash back if he needed to.

"How old are you?"

"Twenty-eight."

Frank's question caught Jesse off guard. "My mother told me that CJ had several women pregnant at the same time. My mother, some rich white bit... quick glance at Jesse, "woman and a girl named Lucy." But I'm 44 years old. It couldn't have been Jesse's mother."

"And I'm 38," Elijah said, locking eyes with his brother. "And Lucy was my mother." The siblings never forgot the look on Elijah's face. From that moment on, Lucy's name was always spoken with respect, if not reverence, by her son's siblings.

Mirembee said, "Jill. Jill has to be one of them." All of them turned towards their sister. "Jesse and I are two years apart, and I've met Carmen. She is only 10. And her mother is not white, light-skinned, but not white. Frank, does your mother know who the other white girl was?"

"I don't know. She didn't say."

"We must talk to her. When can we meet her?

"You can't," Frank said. "My mother ain't getting mixed up in no mess."

"Millions, hundreds of millions," Jesse said.

The meeting with Evelyn Evans was led by Mirembee, who stepped up with expert leadership. The brothers were beginning to accept Mirembee's leadership role that was both assigned and earned, except for Frank. Frank did not accept anyone else's authority, especially a woman, whether she was a sister or not. Evelyn Evans was the guest of honor at one of Cleveland's top five-star restaurants, paid for by Attorney Richard Stock.

Evelyn did not know much. She had heard something about a white girl who lived in the University Heights area. CJ was playing football, and all the girls liked him. I heard that the white girls were always hanging around CJ in school. "He was the star of the football team. I never got to see him play, but the radio man was always saying Williams got the ball. Williams. Touchdown! Williams this and Williams that. I liked hearing his name." Frank noticed that the same smile returned to her face. The same one he remembered when she told him who his father was.

Mirembee interrupted the conversation by asking Evelyn if she knew the names of the other women?

They said he got one pregnant, maybe two besides me. I don't know if it's true or not. He got me, Lucy, and it looks like more. She looked at her son and CJ's other children. "Ya'll have the same eyes," she said.

"Do you have any more names?" Mirembee asked. Jill? Have you ever heard of a Jill?" she added.
Evelyn stated, "Jill? Can't say that I ever heard of no Jill."

"One of the names on the will was Jill. She is one of the…" Mirembee struggled for the right words, "of the…of CJ's children."

"Well, do you know what could have happened to her?" This time, Jesse spoke up.

"Probably the same thing that happened to all dem rich white girls who got babies with black boys back den." Mirembee looked at Frank. "They either got their rich doctor friends to fix it, or they had the babies and gave them up for adoption," Frank added.

"Well, what happened to Jill and her baby?" Jesse repeated.

"Like I said, she either got it fixed or gave it away. I don't know which," Offered Frank.

Mirembee said, "She must have given it away, otherwise, her name wouldn't have been on the will. Thank you, Mrs. Evans."

"Oh, you needn't call me Mrs. Evans. I ain't never been married and the onliest man I ever wanted to marry is dead."

Frank was amazed at the apparent depth of feeling his mother still had for his dead father, and it showed with his raised eyebrows, open mouth, and look of astonishment on his face.

Chapter 24

Attorney Stock

"It's extremely difficult to handle two major lawsuits with the same plaintiffs at the same time," Attorney Stock told the siblings. I suggest we go after Consolidated, get them to settle, and then go for the big fish."

"Consolidated is the big fish," Mirembee inserted. "Their offer of twenty-five thousand is just a sham. Whenever a corporation as big as Consolidated hands out money, something isn't right."

"I believe you are onto something," Stock said. "My investigators have been talking to some employees who worked there about the same time as CJ. It seems the company used a design that CJ developed and has been making big bucks from it."

"How much?" one of the siblings asked.

"We don't know yet, we're still looking into it," Stock said, attempting to redirect their conversation.

"If... if my father's design was worth a lot of money to the company, then he died as a man whose value was quite high. Correct?" Mirembee doggedly continued with the questioning.

"Well. . . yes." Stock agreed.

Sensing that Attorney Stock was beginning to understand, Mirembee said, "A man who died leaving only a dilapidated house, a ten-year-old car, and no money would not be considered an asset to society. His death would not be worth much in the eyes of a judge or jury. But a man who had discovered a new design that was making thousands, maybe millions, for one of the biggest corporations in the US…. in the world, could be worth a hell of a lot of money."

"We'll sue Ohio Gas first..." Stock said, allowing this statement to acknowledge agreement, "and then we will go after the big fish. You all know this is going to cost a lot of money."

"We will use the money we got from the insurance settlement and whatever we get from the gas company."

Yes, and while we are suing them, we will also be putting Consolidated on trial. If you do your job as I expect, Consolidated will settle for what we want when we are ready to go after them," Mirembee reasoned.

"I believe we can do it," Stock said, feeling boosted by Mirembee's expression of trust in him as he shook the hand of each sibling, carefully acknowledging each one by name.

In truth, he did not believe. But he did what he was paid to do and filed a motion in the local court. Once filed, the case of the

Williams siblings was placed among the stacks of papers on Stock's desk.

Chapter 25

Victoria

Victoria Headley was hired by the law firm of Kessler, Stanwick, Stanwick, and Epstein. The Stanwicks were father, Eldon Stanwick, Sr., and son, Eldon Stanwick, II. Eldon the Second married the daughter of Vernon Kessler right out of law school, and he never regretted it. Marrying into the Kessler family was the best career move he could have made. The icing on the cake for Stanwick II was the birth of his son, Eldon III, whom he adored. As a result of Vernon Kessler's untimely death two years ago, Stanwick II was prematurely named a partner.

The three remaining partners retained the Kessler name and appointed Stanwick, Sr. as managing partner, leading a law firm with one hundred attorneys and twice that number in support staff. The firm handled legal matters for some of the largest multinational corporations in the United States and abroad. Each partner and junior associate had membership in the Cleveland Athletic Club and either the Canterbury Golf Club in Beechwood or the Brookside Country Club in Stark County. It was understood that lawyers from a well-respected law firm would wine and dine major clients like Merrill and Merrill Investments, International Communication, and Consolidated Electronic, Inc., using these memberships.

The weekly partners' briefing typically included the four partners, a court reporter, and maybe an assistant or two. Each wore a button-down white shirt and a striped tie with a dark suit. Yellow legal pads rested on the table in front of them and were in the hands of any associates in the room.

Eldon, Sr. noted that a wrongful death lawsuit had been filed against Ohio Gas Company. He assigned the case to his son, Eldon II, to oversee the litigation process with the support of several junior associates handling the paperwork, filing motions, and other tasks. Epstein asked about the nature of the case. Eldon II briefly explained that the deceased was a man, a Black man, whose life was of no consequence.

The lawsuit appears to have been filed by his six illegitimate children. Eldon guessed that the children were probably trying to get some quick money, claiming that Ohio Gas unlawfully shut off his heat, which caused the fire that took his life. He suspected that the siblings would seek a quick and easy settlement.

Everybody is sue-crazy these days. Litigation is second only to the lottery as a get-rich-quick scheme," the elder Stanwick was fond of saying. He always concluded by saying, "And thank God for lawsuits." The men chuckled.

"Lawsuits are better," Epstein said. "Win or lose, we get paid for billable hours." The lawyers responded with laughter. Epstein had a way of reminding his partners that they were in the business of making money from defending their clients against both justified and unjustified lawsuits. Epstein asked if there was any way the company was culpable in the death. "Our clients are always innocent!" Eldon Stanwick, II shot back.

"And it is our job to convince the judge or jury of that fact." Epstein's ability to keep the partners focused earned him high status within the firm. His opinions and legal work were highly respected among practicing and academic legal professionals.

"Epstein, who do you suggest we use as a trial attorney in case it gets that far?"

Prinston. Harry Prinston. First, he's black and he's good. He and that new female attorney we hired last year worked on the Amalgamated case six months ago. As I recall, Amalgamated Systems settled, but it was for a significantly lower amount than any jury verdict would have awarded. Amalgamated was more than satisfied," Epstein said, recalling a case where the firm had to defend a hazardous workplace suit.

Eldon II spoke up. "Her name is Victoria Yale. She's an undergraduate with a law degree and an MBA. Epstein's right. They did an excellent job on that Amalgamated case. But they are both limited when it comes to trying cases. If we go to trial, we'll need someone with more courtroom experience on the team."

"Use Scott Kenny. The three of them ought to be able to kick the asses of a bunch of bastard kids and some unknown lawyer."

Eldon, Sr. Said, "Of course. We'll use Scott. Now, we have a few more cases to assign," concluding the discussion.

One year after graduating from Yale Law School, Victoria earned her MBA, married the man she loved, and secured a prestigious position at a nationally recognized firm. She was happy to be working. After her miscarriage, she went through a period of depression. Now, Victoria suspected she might be pregnant again. Life was good.

The job with Kessler, Stanwick, Stanwick, and Epstein was a godsend. Victoria's salary was three times Will's, although Will's job was seen as a stepping stone to a higher position. Will, Jr. was working in the state's attorney general's office, a foundation for a potentially rising political career, according to Will's father. "Abraham Lincoln was one of several presidents who started out as public attorneys," Will, Sr. told his son. Victoria can earn her income working for Stanwick, and you can start your political journey by being chosen for public practice.

She and Prinston had satisfactorily negotiated the Amalgamated deal. She wanted to go to trial and try the case before a judge and jury, but her client agreed to settle.

"We had a good case, though. I could have won it," she explained to Will Jr. She often discussed her cases with him, and this one was no different. Amalgamated was the defendant in a class-action lawsuit filed by twenty-three migrant workers living in Western Indiana. The migrants charged that Consolidated, the parent company of Aunt Carrie's Jams and Jellies, had violated their civil rights by not providing adequate, safe, and decent housing for the workers on Kohl's Family Farms, Inc. Consequently, an outbreak of hepatitis ravaged the camp. Most of the workers were ill during the picking season and thus lost wages for that season. Health inspectors attributed the spread of the infection to unsanitary conditions, especially water supply and sewage.

It was a typical case of targeting the deepest pockets, Victoria concluded. The lawsuit should have been directed at Kohl's or Aunt Carrie. The workers chose not to sue either of them. Instead, they went after Amalgamated for three hundred thousand dollars and a whopping seven million in punitive and compensatory damages.

The workers settled for one thousand dollars in cash and a new car each for the thirty complainants over eighteen. The idea of the cars came from Scott. He understood that migrant workers relied on transportation to get from one site to another. Victoria handled the negotiations. A new car and cash in hand versus five to ten years tied up in court was a no-brainer for the workers.

The workers' attorneys tried to advise their clients not to accept the settlement. At one point, they brought in Jose Estaves, an important aide to Cesar Chavez, to boost the workers' morale. The settlement money was less than a season's wages, but the automobiles, well, those sealed the deal. She and Scott were congratulated by the partners for their victory. Victoria was proud of her work on the case. She was a little less proud of the hundred-thousand-dollar bonus she received, which was more than the amount earned by the thirty migrants before their attorneys took their share.

Chapter 26
Kate and Carmen

Kate started the discussion. "We want more money, or we walk." Kate didn't see herself as a contract negotiator but as a dedicated mother firmly protecting her child's best interests.

"Mrs. Allison, be reasonable. Ten thousand dollars a week is good money for a child, especially one who isn't even a star."

"Yet!!! You know, and I know, it's just a matter of time before Carmen's name is as famous as Shirley Temple's, Brooke Shields', or even Raven-Symoné's. Pay us now, or you won't be able to afford us later." Kate said with the confidence of a nuclear power. With this statement, Kate was ready to walk out of the offices of Lamba Talent and Production Company (LTP).

"Just a moment, Mrs. Allison. Please sit down. I am sure we can reach a mutual agreement." Kate hoped her feeling of relief wasn't obvious on her face.

From the living room of their leased beachfront villa, Kate called Mirembee. "Is it too late for me, uh, for Carmen to be a part of the lawsuit?" Kate asked after the usual amenities.

"Our lawyers are filing the motions on Monday. They have thirty days to respond. Our lawyers are certain they are going to fight. It could, possibly will, take years before the suit is settled. You want to join us?" Mirembee said, her voice revealing her approval.

"Yes, I, we, it is in Carmen's best interest to be a part of the lawsuit."

"Why?" The question was typical of the new Mirembee, direct and to the point. Kate knew that it would be useless to lie to CJ's child.

I need to secure Carmen's future. Rembee, I like this lifestyle. Carmen likes it too. But I'm being realistic. The money from the trust fund is safe, but everyone gets a piece of revenue from commercials and acting. I never want to go back.

Mirembee respected her honesty. "All right. It's good for us that one child is a minor. I will talk to Attorney Stock tomorrow." Mirembee hesitated and then said, "We still can't find Jill."

"I wish I could help, but I don't know anything. Keep me posted." Kate said.

At ten fifteen, Victoria decided to finish her work for the day. Alongside Scott, she had devoted relentless effort to the case of Williams v. Ohio Gas. Several continuances had given the investigators plenty of time to meticulously prepare comprehensive dossiers for each of the plaintiffs. It's incredible, Victoria thought, these bastard children suing on behalf of their father's estate, which was nearly worthless.

Contrary to the prevailing legal strategy, Victoria and Prinston decided that offense was their best defense. After reviewing the depositions, the pair chose to divide and conquer by challenging the basic claim of the plaintiffs—their alleged paternity.

Besides the handwritten will, the plaintiffs' attorney provided no evidence that Clarence James Williams was the father of any of them, much less all of them. "I don't think this omission is intentional," Victoria said to Prinston during one of the early planning sessions.

"Well, why do you think they did not include documentation which would prove the paternity of the plaintiffs?" Prinston asked.

"It's simple," Victoria explained, "their attorney isn't very bright. I had the research done. Richard Stock is a two-bit shyster. He handles parole violators, DUIs, and petty drug cases. Not much civil work except for a divorce or some other nonsense. In this case, he's way out of his league."

The defense strategy was to admit that Mirembee was Williams' daughter and then challenge the paternity of the others. There was doubt about the paternity of at least three of the remaining five. If the case were to go to a jury — an unlikely outcome based on initial information — they would likely award less money if the number of plaintiffs were fewer.

Next, the defense attorneys were tasked with demonstrating that Clarence James Williams' status in society, both financially and morally, amounted to less than a year's wages at a minimum-wage job. The bastard siblings would be sorry if they refused the $100,000 settlement offer. It would mean they could pocket close to $10,000 each after their shyster attorney got his share.

Finally, they would demonstrate to the jury that Williams' negligence, not Ohio Gas Company, led to his death. The case was neatly wrapped and tied and Victoria was ready to deliver. Tomorrow, she would shock them all by declaring to the judge that she was ready to proceed and that further continuance was not needed.

Chapter 27

Victoria and the mothers

"We call Mirembee Williams to the stand," Stock stated after the two sides completed their opening statements. Responding to Stock's questions, Mirembee recounted the events that led to this day in court. The handwritten will was entered into evidence over Victoria's objection. Victoria allowed Mirembee to testify without objection, except when she referred to her co-plaintiffs as her brothers and sisters.

"Assumes facts not in evidence, your honor," Victoria chimed in. Attorney Stock looked confused, as did Judge Linton. He asked both lawyers to approach the bench. "Your honor, it has not been established that these plaintiffs are indeed the legitimate heirs of Clarence James Williams and, therefore, cannot be referred to as brothers and sisters," Victoria explained.

"Of course, they're brothers and sisters," Stock protested. "The will clearly lists the names of the plaintiffs present here today. They are all the children of Clarence James Williams!"

"Your honor, this alleged will clearly names only one person as the daughter of Clarence James Williams. There is no evidence that the names of other individuals listed are children of Clarence

Williams. They could simply have been witnesses to the signing of this alleged will," Victoria responded.

Judge Linton asked Attorney Stock, "Do you plan to submit additional evidence of paternity? Birth certificates? Marriage licenses? Baptismal records?"

Victoria homed in on the issue. "Until counsel provides this evidence, I submit these plaintiffs should not be referenced as siblings or as the children of Clarence Williams."

"If the court would grant a recess until Thursday, I will provide the evidence, your Honor," Stock was stalling, clearly caught off guard on the first day. Judge Linton agreed not to rule on the objection until he reviewed the evidence. The court was adjourned for the day after thirty minutes of testimony by Mirembee, who could only say that Clarence Williams was married to her mother. She described how the police came to her door to inform her of her father's death.

"Objection," Victoria remained seated but made sure her objection was heard.

"So noted, Mrs. Headley." Judge Linton said.

Stock asked Mirembee several questions about CJ's will. Mirembee explained how she recognized the handwriting as that of CJ's, testifying that, "he named us as his children."

"Move to strike," Victoria demanded.

"Sustained. The jury will disregard Ms. William's last statement."

"Doesn't that prove we are all his children?" Frank posed the question to Attorney Stock during the after-court briefing with the plaintiffs.

Your names are listed in the will but without reference. It's a sensitive matter. We could use more…evidence—birth certificates, baptismal rites, and school reports.

"His name ain't on my fuckin birth certificate," Eli said.

"Mine neither," said Frank.

"Not on mine." Jesse offered when they turned to face him.

"And his name is not on Carmen's or mine," revealed Mirembee. They were surprised by Mirembee's admission. "As a matter of fact, someone else is listed as Carmen's father. How are we going to prove he was our father?" Mirembee asked.

"Our mothers," Jesse offered. "If anyone knows, they do."

"You mean put our mothers on the stand?" Frank asked.

"Yes! Why not?" Jesse said.

"What about me?" Eli slurred. Lucy's death was still a painful memory.

"Someone else must have known. Think about it. Who could testify that CJ was your father?" Mirembee asked.

"Nooo body!" Eli left the room, but not before shouting, "Fuck all of ya'll."

"He'll be back," Jesse's words echoed their thoughts.

"Frank's mother knew about Lucy and the white girl," Mirembee said as Eli slammed the door. Would she be willing to testify?" Mirembee asked, turning to Frank.

The plaintiffs call Evelyn Evans. Frank watched as his mother timidly walked to the witness stand. He remembered the painful conversation it took to get Evelyn here. Exposing her past was not easy for Evelyn. Now that she was a born-again Christian, she had moved past those painful memories. But out of gratitude to CJ and love for Frank, she agreed.

"Please state your name for the court." Attorney Stock began the questioning.

"Evelyn Evans."

"Do you have any children, Mrs. Evans?

"Yes one, Franklin Evans."

"Is he in the court today?"

"Yes."

"Who is Frank's father, Mrs. Evans?"

"Clarence James Williams."

"Objection!" Victoria was on her feet. The witness is stating facts, not in evidence." Judge Linton looked from Victoria to Stock.

"Let's see where this is going." He said, "You may continue Attorney Stock, but I caution you to stick to the evidence."

Stock paused for effect before he continued questioning Evelyn. "Just so I understand. You are saying that you are Franklin Evans' mother, and the late Clarence James Williams is his father?"

"Oh no," Evelyn blurted out, "He ain't late, he dead. But, he sho nuff Franklin's daddy." Even the Judge chuckled audibly.

"Do you know if Clarence James Williams had other children?"

"Yes, I heard. . ."

"Objection, hearsay." Victoria was wasting no time.

"Sustained. Rephrase the question."

"Mrs. Evans, do you have personal knowledge about other children Clarence Williams may have fathered?"

"CJ was married. He and his wife had children, I reckon. I remember he had a woman named Lucy. She was a junkie, but dey had a child. The people say he had some white girls pregnant, but I don't know how many women CJ had. He was a handsome man." Evelyn exhaled, releasing the stress from having to testify.

"Thank you. That's all, your honor."

The decision to let Victoria lead the questioning for the defense was made during a late-night session with the firm's trial attorneys. If they read the jury right, they would not respond well to a man attacking these mothers, regardless of their children's lack of legal status.

Victoria was on her feet immediately. She wasted no time tearing into Evelyn. The investigators hired by her firm had completed dossiers on each of the children and their mothers.

"Mrs. Evans, it is Mrs. Evans, isn't it?" Victoria said, emphasizing Mrs.

"I…I'm not married," Evelyn said.

"Then you are Miss Evans?"

"Yes." Shame caused Evelyn to whisper the answer.

"You'll have to speak up, Mrs…uh, Miss Evans." Judge Linton interjected.

"Miss Evans," Victoria emphasized the Miss, "When was your son born?"

"July 29, 1957"

"Were you married when your son was born?"

"No. I done told you I was not married, ever."

"How old were you when Frank was born?"

"Thirteen."

"And were you a virgin before you. . . "

"Objection. This question is irrelevant, your honor. It has nothing to do with this case." Victoria could have argued the objection, but she chose to stick with her original strategy. "I'll withdraw the question. Miss Evans, since you were not married to Clarence Williams at the time of Franklin's birth, how can you be sure he is the father of your child?"

"Objection."

"Because I knows he is!"

"Wait for the court to rule, Miss. Evans. Overruled. The witness should have direct knowledge of the answer. You may answer."

"I never had nothin' to do with no other man but CJ."

"Miss Evans, did you know Mr. Charles Perkins?" The change in Evelyn's facial expression was obvious to everyone in the court, including the jury. Frank sat straight up in his chair. Mirembee dropped her head. Jesse and Elijah stared. "Miss Evans, was Charles Perkins your stepfather?"

"No, he was my grandmother's man."

"Miss Evans, isn't it true you had sex with him?"

"No! No! No!" Evelyn's sobs erupted from deep inside her. A mix of shame, pity, and remorse shaped her breathing. Something from within made her straighten her shoulders and lift her head. "No, he had sex with me!"

The woman on the witness stand shook even Victoria, but she persisted. Mirembee gripped Frank's hand tight, and Jesse patted him on the back. "How old were you when Mr. Perkins stopped having sex with you?"

"Twelve."

"And how old were you when Frank was born?"

"Thirteen."

"No further questions, your honor."

Stock rose to his feet. "One question for redirect, your honor. Evelyn, do you know why your stepfather stopped sexually abusing you?"

"CJ stopped him."

"Miss Evans, how can you be sure Clarence Williams is Franklin's father?"

"CJ is… was his father. Mr. Perkins ain't bothered me no mo' after CJ. What pruf ya'll needs? Just look at those eyes. Look at all of their eyes. Dey's CJ's eyes." The jury turned to look at the row of defendants.

As his mother left the stand, Frank found himself unable to meet her gaze. A deep rage simmered inside him, directed at CJ, Mirembee, the frustrating lawyers, and anyone else involved in subjecting his mother to this humiliation. No one had the right to treat his mother with such contempt. Nobody could disrespect her like this and get away with it. These fuckers will pay for what they did to his mother, he vowed. The pit of his stomach burned with resentment. In his eyes, no one had the right to treat his mother with such disdain.

"The plaintiffs call Louise Williams Ascot." Money remained the main motivation behind Louise's actions. Mirembee promised Louise more money in addition to repaying the borrowed amount if she testified. Louise was prepared for her testimony, and she challenged anyone to prove Clarence was not Mirembee's father, especially that white bitch lawyer. It was clear that Louise Williams Ascot was not Evelyn Evans.

"Please state your name and address for the court."

"Louise Anderson Williams Ascot, 19402 East Forest Avenue, Shaker Heights, Ohio. Louise tossed her head back and crossed her legs. She was disappointed that the witness stand hid the view of her shapely legs from the jury. She would be sure to emphasize her assets when she left the stand.

"Mrs. Ascot. It is Mrs. Isn't it?"

"Yes, I am the wife of Herbert Ascot," Louise announced.

"Were you married to Clarence James Williams?"

"Yes, I was the only one he married?" Victoria held back on her objection, but Judge Linton didn't. "Just answer the question, Mrs. Ascot. Do not add any additional information."

"Louise turned in the direction of the judge, tossed her hair and smiled, "Whatever you say, your Honor. Mirembee thought she saw the Judge blush.

"Did you and Clarence Williams have any children?"

"Mirembee. Sitting right there looking every bit the spitting image of her daddy."

"Your honor, could you please ask the witness to just answer the questions?" Victoria remained silent as long as she could.

"Mrs. Ascot, please confine your answers to the questions asked."

"Yes. I'm sorry, Judge." Louise's flirtations underscored her apology and did not go unnoticed by the Judge or the jury.

"Mrs. Ascot, were you married to Clarence Williams when Mirembee was born."

"We got married when. . ." Remembering the judge's admonition, she said, "No."

"Is Clarence Williams listed as Mirembee's father on her birth certificate?"

"No."

"Mrs. Ascot, do you have any documents which prove that Clarence Williams is Mirembee's father."

"I sure do."

Louise identified a series of paper documents. The records included baptismal records, insurance policies, bank accounts, school report cards, and non-support papers.

"Thank you, Mrs. Ascot. No further questions. Louise was ready for the white female attorney.

"The defense stipulates that Clarence James Williams is the father of Mirembee Williams." Victoria's formal, crisp voice silenced the courtroom. Obviously disappointed, Louise left the witness stand, intentionally dropping her purse before reaching the observation area. She strategically bent over to pick up the purse, showing the judge and jury the same butt that captured CJ.

The buzz in the courtroom was deafening, though felt rather than heard. Judge, jurors, lawyers, plaintiffs, and spectators visibly showed their shock at Victoria's acceptance of Louise's testimony. No one was more stunned than the Williams children.

"The plaintiffs call Miss Amy Proctor." Stock decided to skip sparring over marital status. "Please state your name and address for the court."

"Amy Proctor. Apartment 6G, 293 Garfield Estates in Cleveland, Ohio." Public housing projects were often named with the word estates at the end.

"Miss Proctor, do you have any children?"

"Yes." This simple answer seemed to strain her intelligence.

"Is Jesse Williams Proctor one of your children?"

"Yes."

"Who is Jesse's father?"

"CJ. I mean, uh, Clarence James Williams."

"Miss Proctor, do you have any documents which prove that Clarence Williams is Jesse's father?"

"I have this letter CJ wrote me after Jesse was born."

"Is this the letter, Miss Proctor?"

"Yes."

"Your honor, could the clerk read the letter, and then we would like it admitted as defense exhibit six." A bit puzzled, the judge agreed when Victoria did not object.

Pretty sweet thing,

You know I love you and our son. I promise you I will do everything I can to help you, the boy, and the other kids, too. Jesse is my son, and I will take care of him. I just won't be seeing you much anymore. I have a wife and daughter. I'm sorry. I am really sorry if I hurt you.

CJ

"That's all, Thank you, Miss Proctor."

Victoria felt guilty about what she was going to do to this small, frail, pathetic creature seated on the witness stand in front of her.

"Miss Proctor, would you read this letter to the jury?" Amy hesitated and squirmed. Jesse knew and felt his mother's humiliation.

"You can read, can't you, Miss Proctor?"

"No, I never learnt how."

"Well, if you can't read, how do you know what the letter says or who wrote it?"

"My son read it to me."

"Your son. You mean Jesse?"

"No, Dennis."

"How many children do you have?"

"I have seven children."

"Is Clarence Williams the father of all of your children?"

"No, jest Jesse."

"Well, who is the father of your other children?"

"Objection, irrelevant, your honor." Stock was searching for a way to stop this line of questioning, having sensed where Victoria was headed. Jesse prayed it would end as well.

"I'll let her answer. You opened the door when you asked that the letter be admitted into evidence."

"Who is the father of your other children, Miss Proctor?"

"They all have different daddies."

"Can you name the six men who fathered your children, Miss Proctor?"

"Yes." Amy got through a list of four men, including CJ, and faltered. The other two last names were Block and Santiago, she knew because she had given her children their father's last names as their middle names.

It was long ago and . . . I can't recall the other two first names. But I gave all of my children dey's fathers last name for a middle name. I jest can't remember dem all." Amy began to cry and Victoria excused her from the stand.

Recovering from the impact of the previous testimony was a significant challenge for Stock. He attempted to gain some relief by requesting that Kate Allison's deposition be admitted as evidence instead of her live testimony. Stock, appearing defeated, explained that Kate's absence in court today was due to urgent business matters. Acknowledging the situation, Victoria expressed no objection, provided that the birth certificate of Carmen deMilo was also admitted along with the deposition. Knowing that Carmen's birth certificate indicated Wayne Edmonson, Sr. as Carmen's father, Stock wanted to object to its inclusion. However, he also realized Victoria had him. "We accept both documents, your honor," a very compliant Stock said.

"No objection." Victoria, sensing victory, stated.

Victoria's stunning performance during the first week of the trial won accolades from the partners. Even her co-counsels, Stinson and Kenny, congratulated and applauded her. They were so happy with how she handled the case that the partners made her lead counsel.

Victoria's elation over being appointed lead counsel was shared with Will over a glass of bourbon for him and lemon-flavored Perrier for her.

After an hour of passionate lovemaking, Victoria gently placed Will's hand on her abdomen. "Our baby is moving," she said to a now sleeping Will. Her eyes closed with a smile on her face.

Chapter 28
Blood Lines

Glasses with ice and bourbon tinkled as four of the Williams' children and their attorney discussed the day's court session. Mirembee and Jesse refused the hard liquor and nursed colas, while Eli was on his third drink, and Frank accepted a double shot of Wild Turkey. Stock tried to put a positive spin on the testimonies, but whatever he was selling, they weren't buying. Finally, Mirembee asked, "Could a blood test or a medical test prove CJ was our father?"

Eli said, "Apparently, sista, you don't need any goddam proof." His slurred voice showing the effects of the bourbon. Mirembee wondered how long before this ticking bomb would explode again.

"Look," Jesse said, "She, that attorney, is trying to divide us. We can't let that happen. Listen to what Rembee has to say." Rage can only be subdued momentarily, so Eli was still for now.

"Can a blood test prove he is our father?"

"He's dead. Where are you going to get his blood from?"

"We could exhume the body." Even the thought of an exhumation was emotionally draining for Mirembee. But the new Mirembee was determined.

"He's fuckin dead." reiterated Frank, the only one who did not feel any positive emotion towards CJ. "They embalmed him. He ain't got no blood."

"We do." offered Jesse. Mirembee knew Jesse's mind was slow, but she marveled at how he was always able to see the obvious. Stock was the first to respond.

"He's right! The defense has already stipulated that Clarence is Mirembee's father. All we have to do is provide evidence that you are all related."

"Is that possible?" Mirembee was skeptical.

"We will know soon. Dr. David Gardner is an expert geneticist. He won't be cheap, but I will have our investigator contact him."

"Will we have enough time? To contact him? To put him on the stand?" Mirembee asked.

"Yes. I can always present expert witnesses." Tomorrow, we will put the Consolidated officials on the stand." Stock's attempt to accentuate the positive continued.

"Before the gas company?"

"Yes."

"I just want to know how that bitch knew about Greatgram's husband? I didn't even know until a few days ago. And ya'll the only ones I told." Frank slurred.

"Victoria?" The telephone call startled her, and she awoke before Will, who was a heavy sleeper, to answer it.

"Yes.'

"You heard of Dr. David Gardner?"

"Who is this?"

"Just listen, bitch. You heard of him?"

"Nooo. . . "

"Well, you will. They're going after Consolidated tomorrow."

"Why…?"

"You ought to be able to figure that out, smart lady." The caller hung up, revealing no further information. This was the second time the mysterious caller had woken Victoria in the middle of the night. The caller was right about the plaintiffs' attempt to prove paternity by putting the mothers on the stand. Overtime pay convinced her investigators to work around the clock. That piece of dirt about Evelyn Evans' step-grandfather was worth the one thousand dollar-a-day charge.

Victoria stayed awake for the rest of the night. She hadn't told her co-counsel anything about the mystery caller. At first, she thought it was just a prank, but she soon realized he was right about the mothers testifying. It was clear that the caller was someone on the other side. But who? Definitely not someone working for Stock. One of the siblings? Why?

Morning found Victoria no closer to an answer. Victoria chose to blame her pregnancy for the feeling that gnawed at her gut, warning of some impending disaster. Although shaken, she decided to continue with her defense strategy, attacking the character of Clarence James Williams, his children's mothers, and the children themselves.

Chapter 29

Williams v Myers

"The plaintiffs call Mr. Wilson Myers to the stand."

"Objection, your honor, the defense fails to see what purpose this witness serves," shot Victoria. Stock argued that Wilson Myers could establish Clarence James Williams's value to Consolidated Electronic and thus help the jury determine a monetary value for his heirs to compensate for his loss. Victoria wanted Myers to hear this explanation before he testified, so despite knowing Stock was predicting a win with this explanation to the judge, Victoria let the testimony proceed without further objections.

As he waited for the judge to rule, Myers looked at Mirembee and remembered her last words to him, 'screw you.' How dare this bastard child of a nobody talk to the CEO and President of Consolidated Electronics this way. Who the fuck did she think she was? He offered her twenty-five thousand dollars, more money than she had ever seen in her life, and she said, 'screw you.' Well, we will see who gets screwed now.

"Mr. Myers? Mr. Myers?" Stock's voice brought him back to the present. "Please state your name and position for the court." Other preliminary questions followed, with Myers responding as succinctly and perfunctorily as possible. Stock was respectful and precise in asking about CJ's employment with the company. The questions were genteelly put, causing Wilson Myers to relax his guard just a bit. Sensing this, Stock zeroed in.

"Have you met Miss Mirembee Williams?"

"Yes"

"Did you request a meeting with Miss Williams?"

"No, she called me."

"Did she call you as a result of a letter you wrote?"

"Yeess."

"Is this the letter?" Stock said, handing a copy to Victoria and one to the clerk.

"Wilson Myers put on his glasses and slowly read the letter. Stock waited as if time was of no consequence.

Finally, Myers answered, "Yes."

"Please read this letter for the court." Again, Myers complied with Stock's request.

Stock: "So, Miss Williams telephoned you after she received your letter?" Now, Myers was beginning to feel uneasy.

Myers: "The letter was written to Clarence James Williams. She said she was his daughter."

Stock: "How would you characterize the discussion at that meeting?"

Myers: "It was a cordial meeting." Myers was not going to help him. If he wanted information, then he had better ask the right questions.

Stock: "Mr. Myers, at that meeting, did you offer Miss Williams twenty-five thousand dollars?"

Myers: "Yes."

Stock: "Why?"

Myers: "It was money Consolidated owed Clarence Williams."

Stock was beginning to get impatient with the cat and mouse game. "Why did Consolidated owe Clarence Williams money?"

Myers: "He left without collecting his last paycheck."

Stock: "So, Mr. Williams was an assembly line worker making twenty-five thousand dollars a month."

Myers: "No. The company was paying him interest on the money we owed him."

Stock: "Mr. Myers, will you please tell the court if the money you offered Miss Williams included payment for anything else besides Mr. Williams' last paycheck and any interest accrued to it?"

Myers hesitantly: "Yes."

Stock: "Yes, what? Mr. Myers"

Myers: "It included other payments."

Stock: "What was the other payment for?"

Myers: "A suggestion he made."

Stock: "Is that all, Mr. Myers?"

Myers: "I was not CEO at the time Mr. Williams was employed by Consolidated."

Stock: "Your honor, please instruct the witness to answer the question." Stock's patience was hanging on a thin line.

"You must answer the question, Mr. Myers." Myers looked at Victoria, then Mirembee, and then the brothers.

Myers: "No, that wasn't all." Stock waited to see if he needed to keep asking for more answers from Myers. "Part of the money was a contribution to his estate for a device he invented while working at Consolidated."

Stock: "Was this device a circuit adapter?"

Myers: "Yes."

Stock: "And did Consolidated use this device in the production of electronic boards?"

Myers: "Yes."

Stock: "Mr. Myers, how much money was generated for Consolidated as a result of Mr. Williams' invention?"

Myers: "That's difficult to determine."

Stock: "Would one million dollars be in the ballpark?"

Myers shifted his weight, adjusted his tie and used his index finger to push his glasses closer to his eyes. "One million would be in the ballpark."

Stock circled, stocking his prey and narrowed in. "Would ten million dollars be closer to home plate, Mr. Myers?"

Myers looked at the judge and decided to answer truthfully. "Yes."

Stock: "Mr. Myers, please tell this jury if Consolidated posted an increase of one hundred million dollars in sales after using the circuit adapter invented by Mr. CJ Williams?"

Myers: "There were many reasons why our sales increased. Stock prices rose, we acquired two new manufacturing plants, and the union agreement permitted as much overtime as necessary."

Stock: "And the circuit adapter?"

Myers: "Yes. It was a small part of the increase."

Stock: "So the circuit adapter could be credited with increasing profits somewhere between one million and one hundred million dollars?" Even in defeat, Myers walked the tightrope.

"Not exactly." Stock left the answer stand, figuring the jury was smart enough to accept the answer for what it was.

Stock: "Mr. Myers, do you recognize this document?" A ten-page document written in small type and filled with legalese was handed to Myers.

Myers' heart sank when he recognized the document. He cursed himself for letting the Williams bitch leave with the settlement papers. Why didn't he call security and stop her like he wanted? Then he remembered his secretary arrived early that day and was ready to serve him. Damn! He thought, one hundred-million-dollar blowjob.

Myers: "This is the settlement paper our attorney wrote to clear up the Williams' matter."

Stock: "Mr. Myers, will you read the highlighted portion for the jury?"

Myers: ". . . in lieu of any claims against the company, Mr. Clarence James Williams will receive a monetary sum of twenty-five thousand dollars." Myers broke his own rule and added, "The invention belonged to the company. He invented it on company time. We didn't have to offer him anything." He immediately regretted the statement.

Stock: "Mr. Myers, when was Clarence Williams employed at Consolidated?"

Myers shifted through some papers before answering, "From May 8, 1985, through December 4, 1991."

Stock: "Mr. Myers, will you please identify this document for the court?"

Myers: "It appears to be from the US Patent Office."

Stock: "It is from the U. S. Patent Office, Mr. Myers. It is a patent granted to Clarence James Williams for his invention of circuit adapter #06321. What is the date on the patent, Mr. Myers?"

Even the judge wondered why Victoria had allowed Myers to be questioned relentlessly by Stock. Surely, she would object to any reference Myers made to a document he had no direct knowledge of. Myers was pissed. Victoria was saving her client and sacrificing him and Consolidated in the process. Stock was quietly ecstatic; the jury was his, the big battle was won, and he was the victor. Even the Williams children were beginning to respect him.

Myers: "Our personnel records indicate that he was arrested on April 4, 1991. He did not report to work after that."

Stock: "Thank you Mr. Myers. That is all."

"Does the defense which to cross?" Judge Linton directed his question to Victoria.

Victoria: "According to this report, CJ Williams was arrested while working for your company. Do your records indicate the charge for which he was arrested?"

Myers: "Yes."

Victoria: "And what was the charge?"

Myers: "Non-payment of child support."

Victoria: "Mr. Myers, is this a copy of Mr. Williams' employment file with your company?" Stock was on his feet to object when Victoria offered him a copy.

Myers inspected the documents and answered, "Yes."

Victoria: "Please refer to his initial employment application. Does it list any dependents?"

Myers: "Yes."

Victoria: "How many?"

Myers: "Three."

Victoria: "Whose names are listed?"

"Clarence James Williams, Louise Williams and Mirembee Williams.

Victoria: "Will you please remove his life insurance application? Does he list any beneficiaries?"

Myers: "Mirembee Williams."

Victoria: "Does your company provide health care for your employees?"

Myers: "Yes, and dental, too, if they sign up for it."

Victoria: "Did Clarence Williams request any or both of those insurance coverages?"

Myers: "Yes."

Victoria: "Whose names are listed for coverage?"

Myers: "Clarence, Louise and Mirembee Williams."

Victoria: "Mr. Myers, did Clarence Williams complete an E form?"

Myers: "Yes."

Victoria: "How many dependents did he list for income tax purposes?"

Myers: "Three."

Victoria: "And those names are?"

Myers: "Clarence, Louise and Mirembee Williams."

Victoria: "Mr. Myers, are there any documents in that file listing the names of additional children or other dependents?"

Myers: "No."

Victoria: "Thank you, Mr. Myers. I have one more question. Do your records indicate who filed the non-support complaint?"

Myers: "Yes."

Victoria: "Who was the complainant?"

Myers: "Mrs. Louise Ascot."

Victoria: "No further questions."

"I say we git that bitch!" Eli and his liquor were talking.

"You mean smoke her?" Frank asked.

"Hold on now, I can't even listen to this conversation, let alone be a part of it," Stock said, having no doubt Eli and Frank were capable of executing a lethal solution to this problem.

"No, he means do to her what she's doing to us," Mirembee said.

"How we going to do that?" asked Jesse.

"We can have HER investigated," explained Mirembee.

"Exactly how's that going to help us, little sista.?" Frank threw a skeptical look at Mirembee.

Victoria's skilled performance in court acted as a catalyst, deepening the growing divide among the Williams siblings. Recognizing how crucial it was to keep her brothers' support, Mirembee understood that the possibility of Ohio Gas offering her a settlement alone, excluding her siblings, could jeopardize any future agreement with Consolidated. The complex family dynamics now hung in the balance, with Mirembee carefully balancing her personal interests against the unity of her brothers and sisters.

"I don't know, but everybody has secrets, something they don't want anybody to know. Maybe she does too," Mirembee said.

I'll put Burly on it, but I have to admit, this is costing a lot of money; he's already working on finding your missing sister. Burly will want more money, Stock informed them.

"We can get the money from Kate. Tell him to do it." Mirembee had spoken.

Chapter 30

Burly

Burly was not a typical private detective. Even his name was a misnomer. Burly C. May was a former high school teacher. Throughout his thirty years teaching literature, he remained fascinated by mystery novels. Solving murders and uncovering the killer from potential suspects before the author revealed their identity were his passions.

After a year of retirement inactivity, Burly opened a storefront office in a seedy part of town called The Flats. Burly ignored the landlord's obvious amusement when he explained that he was a private investigator. With his state-issued license, Burly convinced the landlord that he was legitimate and capable of paying the monthly rent.

Burly still looked and dressed like a schoolteacher. A plaid vest, an open shirt collar, and generally brown trousers slick from wear were his standard uniform. He carried 160 pounds on his six-foot frame. The noise about him being gay was just that…noise. Burly didn't give a damn what they said. He liked his hair long. His slightly built frame, horn-rimmed glasses, and a pencil always tucked behind his ear enhanced the teacher's image, making his role as a private detective seem suspicious. His outward appearance concealed the inner genius behind the glasses.

Burly was not motivated by money; sure, he needed a paycheck to cover the bills, since his meager retirement check didn't quite do the job, but his true motivation came from the satisfaction he felt whenever he cracked a case.

Working on the Williams case was proving to be very unsatisfying. All he had to go on was the first name Jill from Clarence's will, and Evelyn's recollection of a rich white girl called Silly Jilly. There were eighteen Jills in the high school yearbooks, including CJ Williams. Burly had vigorously pursued each name and came up empty. Now, they wanted him to investigate Victoria McMillen Headley. At least he had a full name, and the woman was alive. He knew where she lived, her parents' names, her husband and his family, her employers, and the schools she attended. Her complete vita was easily accessible from the Yale University Placement Center. This should be straightforward. It wasn't.

Nothing Burly discovered would be useful to Stock and his clients. This woman was clean—too clean, maybe. There had to be something he was overlooking. A trip to the Cuyahoga County Health Department vital statistics archives provided a clue. To Burly's surprise, the county recorded the births of two Victoria Lynn McMillens. Both were born in 1958 and within six months of each other, to the same parents. The proverbial lightbulb went off in Burly's head. He switched from the birth records to the death records. There was a death certificate for the Victoria born on May

24, 1958. Parents who had lost one child might name the second in her honor, but not six months later, he thought. The time constraints cast doubt on the possibility of a full-term pregnancy, given the circumstances of this second birth. Retrieving the second birth certificate from his pocket, the details spoke volumes: seven pounds, six ounces, nineteen inches. The meticulous records suggested a full-term baby. While Agatha Christie's fictional Dr. Perot might enjoy unraveling such mysteries, this was Burly's case, and he was determined to solve it.

The second Victoria had to be adopted. Maybe this was what he was searching for. In the 1950s, adoption records were sealed. Finding an adoptive child's birth parents would be challenging— the kind of case that made Burly's mouth water. The only question was where to start.

Stock chose to call supervisors and co-workers of CJ to the stand after Wilson Myers' testimony. He had won the jury over with Myers, but the extra testimony would help solidify his case. He decided to stop after two supervisors and ten co-workers testified. Victoria was relentless, getting his co-workers to admit that while Clarence bragged about being a ladies' man, he never admitted to having more than one child.

Victoria focused on Clarence's tendency to exaggerate. 'He was always bragging about somethin',' was a common response from coworkers. No, he didn't always pay his bills on time. Yes, he could have paid the bills. He always had lots of money. No, he never mentioned any kids besides Rembee. Yes, he drank at least a half pint a day, but so did most of the guys on the line. No, I never saw him drunk, but he usually had a pint of Canadian Club in the trunk of his car. Indeed, women found him appealing. However, I cannot recall any mention of a girlfriend. Nevertheless, I distinctly remember seeing the police place handcuffs on him and then take him away.

Stock described their testimony as a toss-up. They didn't help, but they also didn't hurt the case. After a brief break for the Christmas holiday, Stock told his clients that the gas company officials would be next to testify.

"It looks like our sister is going to be a very rich woman," Eli added with as much sarcasm as his alcohol-laden mind would allow.

"Dammit, Eli, can't you see Rembee isn't about to leave us out?" Jesse swore, catching everyone off guard.

Eli retaliated, "Yeah, wait until they offer her a nice fat settlement."

Eli was a prophet, thought Stock. He was expecting a call from Victoria any day now. Moreover, he reasoned that Eli was correct. The offer would be for Mirembee. The brothers, Carmen and whoever Jill was, would be left out if Mirembee decided to take the money and run. Stock was not convinced she would divide with the other siblings. Why should she? Victoria had been quite successful in establishing the fact that evidence proving CJ had fathered the other children was not convincing. Mirembee could walk away with a cool million or more. His share, of course, excluded.

"What has Burly found out? And what about the geneticist?" Mirembee asked.

Blood tests can show a match, but paternity would still be doubtful. I'm not sure we want to go down that path," Stock said. "I expect to hear from Burly this afternoon.

"Burly, goddamn it, what have you got?" Stock yelled into the phone. Stock hesitated; he hadn't heard from Burly since requesting the information on Victoria. "Are you still working on both investigations?" "When can I expect something, anything? Time is running out. What do you have?"

"Give me a couple more days, I'm on to something." Burly pleaded, knowing he was no closer to finding the missing sister than he was yesterday, the day before, or last week.

Burly's break came unexpectedly as he was walking home from his office. Neighborhood children were playing jump rope when an argument suddenly broke out. One little girl yelled at the other, 'We ain't afraid of you, Hairy Mary.' Burly stopped in his tracks. He knew this little girl whom the children called Hairy Mary. Her mother always called her by her full name, Harriet Marie. The kids called her Hairy Mary, a pun on her real name. Children often did that to tease each other. They would take the child's real name and turn it into a silly rhyme. Silly Jilly, Silly Jilly, Silly Jilly.

Burly nearly tripped on the steps leading to his rented storefront office. Without removing his coat, he hurried to his file cabinet located directly behind the old schoolteacher desk he bought at the school district's annual used furniture auction. Locking and unlocking the cabinet every day took time, but he believed the security was necessary. So, he carefully made sure it was closed every evening before leaving his office. Now, the lock was keeping him from its contents and slowing down his progress.

Once opened, a quick search yielded the boldly labeled file of Clarence James Williams. The dossier Burly had compiled on CJ was exhaustive but incomplete. Clarence was born and raised in Cleveland, Ohio. He attended his local neighborhood elementary and high school until the eleventh grade. Clarence Williams transferred to Cleveland Heights High School during his junior year. Burly reasoned that this was due to the federal government's requirement to desegregate Cleveland Public Schools.

By 9:00 a.m. the next morning, Burly sat in the parking lot, waiting for the public library doors to open. Since Burly was the only patron in the reference section, the clerk gladly assisted him find five years' worth of University Heights yearbooks and placed them on the table in front of him. With surgical precision, Burly scanned the pages. What he was looking for he didn't know.

Burly seldom let his mind wander, but after thirty minutes of studying every student's picture in four yearbooks, his thoughts kept returning to the classroom. Football and basketball players, the jocks, weren't interested in literature, no matter how hard he tried to make his class current and relevant. Occasionally, an adventure novel or a novel with a young hero could catch their attention, but Burly didn't consider those novels as real literature.

Female students, especially those on the honor roll, always enjoyed love and mystery novels. Unfortunately, Burly's current case did not involve adventure, love, or mystery. Or maybe it did, thought Burly, turning back to the yearbooks, only this time focusing on the activity pictures.

Among the two Black players on the squad, it was easy to pick out Williams. That's it, Burly told himself. Think like a high school football star, not just any high school football player, but a Black stand-out player in an almost all-white school. What does a player like that want? He corrected himself. Who does a player like that want? The prettiest, most popular girl in school whom everybody has the hots for, but the white boys hadn't been able to approach.

Burly searched the pictures of all the female high school seniors, hoping to find a connection.

When he finished with the seniors, he moved on to the juniors. Halfway through, his eyes locked on the name Ann (Silky) Gillian. Nicknames of each student were placed in parentheses between their first and last names. Silky . . . Silly, Gillian. . . Jilly. Burly was on fire. He searched for more pictures of this girl and found plenty. Her photo was among others on the cheerleading squad, the newspaper staff, candy striper volunteers, Future Teachers of America, and President of the Junior Class.

What Burly couldn't understand was the lack of any record of Ann Gillian in the next yearbook when she should have been a senior. It was as if she had vanished into thin air.

Seeking more information, Burly decided to check newspapers from that time. After navigating two hours of ancient news, he hit pay dirt. Ann Gillian was one of the cheerleaders interviewed after the Cleveland Heights Tigers' big win over archrival Shaker Heights.

If he hurried, he could still make it to the county office before it closed. The county clerk wasn't as helpful as the librarian, but he retrieved the public records and told Burly how to find the information he needed.

Although hiring someone to conduct a title search was an option, time constraints prevented Burly from taking that route. Undeterred by this limitation, his unwavering investigative efforts revealed that the Gilliams were no longer living at the address listed in the newspaper. Their home at 11324 Beechcliff was sold to Vivian and Joseph McIntosh. Fortunately, the transfer deed listed the Gilliams' new address as Houston, Texas.

At four fifteen, the nondescript clerk told him that the office would close in fifteen minutes. That's the problem with this country, pondered Burly. Government bureaucrats and teachers—they all leave at four thirty, whether the work is completed or not. When he was a teacher, it was common for him to stay in his classroom well past eight P.M., diligently grading papers or preparing lesson plans for the next day.

The transition from the public library to the county office building and back again was smooth. Walking from the pillared county building to the historic century-old public library across the street took less than five minutes, and the library was open from nine to nine.

He quickly jotted down the numbers of the three Harold Gilliams listed in the Houston telephone directory. This time, luck was his backup. His first call was the right one. He hated lying and only did it when it was necessary. "I'm trying to locate Silky. I mean Ann, concerning our high school reunion. My name is…" he picked a name from the yearbook, praying that they had not kept in touch, "Bill Daniels."

"Yes, I remember you. This is Ann's mother."

"How have you been, Mrs. Gilliam?"

"Just fine. I'm sorry about your mother. We heard about it too late to come to the funeral."

This is why Burly hated lying. One lie always led to another. "Thank you, Mrs. Gilliam, it was extremely hard on the family. We are doing better now."

"Your father remarried, didn't he?"

"Yes. Mrs. Gilliam, do you know how I can get in touch with Ann?" Burly wanted to end this part of their conversation quickly.

"Sure, dear, she lives in Seattle with her husband. Hold on, I'll get her address and telephone number for you. You know, I've thought of remarrying."

Burly hung up the phone immediately after getting the information he needed. Within five minutes, he called the airline's reservation desk. By 9:00 AM the next morning, he was on a plane heading for Seattle.

Chapter 31
Victoria's Skeletons

"You better not have any skeletons in your closet, counselor."

"Listen, who are you?" This time, the volume in her voice caused Will to stir.

"Don't matter. Have I been right so far?"

The caller always called during the wee hours of the morning when her thinking was not clear, and her mind was not at full capacity.

"If you got skeletons, you better get rid of them," he hung up. Victoria pulled the covers up to her neck. She turned toward her husband, letting her stomach touch the small of his back. Her baby kicked, and she prayed. Of course, he would still love her. Many people were adopted. Surely, it would not matter to her beloved Will that her father was black. She had not changed; she was still the same person. He had to love her and their baby. Tomorrow, she would talk to her mother. Who was this caller so bent on destroying her life over what—a lawsuit, a million-dollar lawsuit? People have done much worse for much less, she thought.

Jesse hung up the telephone and returned to the bed he and Mirembee shared. Mirembee could not believe what she had just learned. Jesse! Jesse was the traitor! Jesse called the white attorney and revealed their plans. Jesse is the traitor.

Both lay awake, unable to sleep. Jesse's mind raced with reasons for his actions. Why was he trying to hurt Rembee? CJ wanted him and Rembee to be a family, to live together as brother and sister. That was the problem. CJ wanted Rembee to have a family, not Jesse. He didn't care at all about Jesse. Everything was for Rembee—Rembee's pictures, Rembee's birthday party, Rembee's new dress, Rembee's report card. Rembee, Rembee, Rembee. Now, Rembee was going to get everything. Jesse and the others would be left holding their crotches in their hands. But Rembee would be rich. Well, not if he could help it. Not this time.

Mirembee kept pretending to sleep, but her mind was racing. Jesse, not Jesse. Why Jesse? She had thought it was Eli at first and then dismissed him. Then it had to be Frank; he didn't care about CJ and didn't care who knew it. But Jesse, why? Sleep wouldn't come. She got up early and headed to Stock's office before work.

Chapter 32
Ann Gilliam Coulter

Burly knocked on the door of the multi-story modern home in the exclusive bayfront neighborhood of Seattle. An absolutely stunning woman in her forties, dressed in black Capri pants and a white silk T-shirt, greeted him.

"Are you Ann Gillian?"

"Well, I used to be," she flashed a smile that made the down payment on some orthodontist's new Jaguar. "Now I am Mrs. Steven Coulter." Burley felt he was supposed to recognize the name, but he did not. He decided not to lie.

"My name is Burly. I am a private investigator from Ohio. May I ask you a few questions?" Without waiting for an answer, Burly asked, "Did you know a Clarence Williams?"

Ann rushed outside, shutting the door behind her. Her smile was instantly replaced with a look of despair. She seemed unable to stop the quivering of her bottom lip or the rapid blinking of her eyes. Burly felt she was about to... to collapse right there at the front entrance.

"What do you want?" Ann asked, shaking but able to gather her thoughts enough to speak. Burly softened his tone. "I just want to talk to you. Is there somewhere we could go?"

"No, I can't... there is no place,…my husband, my children…" Ann was holding back tears.

"I'm not here to hurt you, but we must talk. Fifteen minutes, that's all I need. We will talk now or later, Mrs. Coulter." Burly was not going to let this fish wiggle off the hook.

"Tomorrow then. I meet you in town," Ann offered.

"Today, Mrs. Coulter. Now."

Ann felt trapped. The moment she had dreaded all her adult life had arrived. A past that had haunted her since her sixteenth year was now haunting her again. "Toshi, bring me the keys to the . . . van." Burly determined she had a choice of cars and chose the most nondescript one. "Wait for me at the corner, and then follow me," she whispered to Burly, who obeyed without questioning.

He was sure Ann had no plans to try to escape now. As he headed to his car, he overheard her telling the unseen Toshi that she needed new makeup for the upcoming evening. A face like that didn't need any makeup. He wondered if the invisible Toshi brought the story.

She drove for fifteen minutes and stopped in front of a sportswear store, a strange place for a private meeting, thought Burly. He exited his car and started toward her. She shook her head to caution him not to approach her. The clerk greeted her by name and asked if he could show her something. Ann loudly declared, "I'm going to the steam room at the spa. I'll need some sandals and a skin moisturizer." Burly took the hint and purchased swim trunks and water shoes.

They left the store with their purchases and headed to the spa. Ann passed him at the entrance and whispered, "Wait five minutes and come into the steam room." Ingenious thought, Burly. Based on the number of people who greeted her, Burly figured she was very well known throughout the town, or at least at this spa.

Burly entered the steam room and noticed Ann and two others through a cloud of steam. Ann waited patiently until the others left and said to Burly, "What do you want?"

"I want to talk to you about Clarence Williams. But…" Burly was having difficulty breathing.

"I will tell you what you want to know, but I do not want to meet her. It was the best decision at the time." Ann confessed.

Burly sensed that Ann had anticipated this moment for some time and was now saying her well-rehearsed lines. He decided to play along. "So, you do not want to meet her?"

With the steam cloud gone, Burly could see her face clearly. She looked like a small, fragile child rather than the middle-aged woman she was, admitting to taking the last cookie from the jar. "Of course not. My parents' lawyers handled everything about the adoption. They said the adoptive family was wealthy. Their baby had died six months earlier, and the wife was so depressed that the officials wouldn't allow them to adopt through the usual process. The lawyers said they would be happy to…" The door opened, and two very thin women entered the room. Ann smiled and asked, "How's the sauna?"

"Dry and hot," one of the females said.

This time, Burly was the first to leave. The sauna was just a few steps away. Ann stepped under a cold-water shower between the two rooms. Unaccustomed to the health club routine, Burly skipped the shower and went straight into the sauna. Burly's skin felt like it was being pricked by a million needle points. This was one interview he would never forget. He was glad no one else was there.

Once they were alone, Burly took a chance and asked, "Did Clarence consent to the adoption?" He was starting to connect the dots.

"Clarence was a poor black boy from Cleveland, he was never even asked. He knew I was pregnant, though."

"Tell her I loved her, but I couldn't. I just couldn't keep her. The lawyers promised she would have a good life. My parents paid them a lot of money to manage the adoption. She has a good life, doesn't she?" More than an answer, Ann wanted a confirmation of her decision.

"Yes," Burly answered, reluctant to tell her the truth and wishing he didn't have to lie. "I have two more questions. What was the name of the lawyers who handled the adoption?"

"They were Jewish, uh, Cline and Horowitz or something like that. I think."

"And the name of the family who adopted her?" Burly asked before thinking.

Ann stood on her feet and, for the first time, looked directly into the eyes of this intrusion on her life and demanded, "Didn't she tell you that?"

Lying has a way of catching up with you. Burly decided to tell the truth. "Mrs. Coulter, your daughter did not send me here to find you."

"Who? And who are you?"

"I told you. I am a private investigator. I work for the six children of Clarence James Williams who are suing Ohio Gas on behalf of Clarence Williams' estate."

"He's dead?"

"Yes. It's a wrongful death civil action. The other children need to find your daughter since she is a plaintiff in the suit."

"How did they know?"

"CJ, Clarence left a will."

The two females entered the sauna. Ann did not stop talking, "Was he rich?"

"No." Burly became edgy over the presence of the two outsiders.

"Why did he leave a will?" The two females turned to hear the man's answer.

"It's hot in here," he said. They left the sauna together and walked to the poolside.

Seated on the white plastic chairs, Ann repeated her question, "Why would CJ leave a will?"

"I don't know, but the other children have been located. He simply listed the name Jill for your daughter, and I am trying to locate her."

Ann was quiet for a moment, then said, "Don't! Nothing good can come from it. Let sleeping dogs lie." She rose from the chair and turned to leave, the imprint of the white plastic still on the back of her thighs. "I never want to see you again!" she said.

Chapter 33

Burly

Burly was a man possessed. His mind matched the engine of the airplane returning Burly to Ohio—both running at full power. Armed with information from Ann, Burly was determined to find the missing daughter. Stock's demands to dig up dirt on the white female lawyer could wait, but to play it safe, he decided to put all his cards on the table.

Capitalizing on his training as an educator, Burly decided to tackle both problems at the same time. He often told his students to start by separating the knowns from the unknowns. Burly drew up an outline for both cases. Known facts were:

(Jill) Daughter	(Victoria) Attorney
female	female
age approx 25	age 26
Parents then not known	adopted
Bio mother – Ann Gilliam	Bio mother – unknown
Bio father - CJ Williams	Bio father – unknown
Adoptive Parents - unknown	Adoptive Parents- J Clyde/Clara McMillian
Residence - Ohio	Residence- Ohio to New Haven back to Ohio

Seeing the two lists side by side puzzled Burly. That strange feeling that churns in your gut when something seems off, not quite right, gripped him. No way, he thought. It couldn't be. It had to be a coincidence. He listed the unknowns and unanswered questions:

1. Who were Victoria's biological parents?

2. Who handled the adoptions?

3. Why did the attorney charge so much money for Victoria's adoption?

Burly knew he couldn't access adoption records without a court order. His best chance was through the lawyers. He did thorough research on the law firm before calling for an appointment. This time, he told the truth. He explained to the receptionist that he wanted to speak with an attorney about an adoption. The junior clerk he met was newly out of law school, which Burly expected. In the 1960s, Cline, Horowitz & Stein, LLC was made up solely of the three attorneys whose names were on the office door. Over the past fifteen years, the firm had grown significantly, and now about thirty attorneys occupied the offices and cubicles on the entire third floor of the Johnson building.

"You wanted to see an attorney about an adoption, Mr. May. How can we help you?" the young attorney asked with an obvious intent to assist.

"You can help me by telling Mr. Cline and Mr. Horowitz I am here about the Gilliam adoption," Burly answered, crisp and clean.

"I don't understand. Is this about an adoption that has already taken place, Mr. May? Adoption records are sealed. We cannot give you any information regarding an adoption this firm may or may not have been involved with." The lawyer responded with less enthusiasm than before.

"Young man, you have landed a very good job here. I suggest you give this card to your senior partners and tell them I can be reached at this number. Then maybe you'll be able to continue working here. Without waiting for a response, Burly left and returned to his office. Fifteen minutes after he was seated at his desk, the telephone rang as he expected.

"Mr. May, Levi Horowitz. I understand that you wanted to talk to someone about an adoption."

"That's correct, Mr. Horowitz. I want to know where the money went." Burly went straight for the jugular.

"What money?"

"The money you collected from the family, or should I say families?" added Burly.

"It's best if we discuss this matter in person. Why don't you come to our office say 2:00?"

Sensing he had hooked the fish, Burly wanted to reel it in before it got away. "No, why don't you come to my office, say 1:00?"

"Very well, we can meet at Rolando's. I have a private room there. It's located…"

I know where it is. 1:00. Burly knew the meeting was going to be difficult. Getting lawyers to speak plainly was hard enough and having them admit to involvement in a possible illegal adoption scheme was nearly impossible. Still, it was his only chance to unravel this mystery.

The three men in suits introduced themselves as Levi Horowitz, Steven Cline, and Robert Herald. Burley was straightforward. He needed to know the names of the adoptive family for the Gillian child. They took turns explaining the legalities of adoption and how records were sealed, and private matters could not be made public. Burly was ready for them. He reasoned that the attorneys had accepted money from both sides to complete arrangements for the adoption. Perhaps they could convince a judge that their actions were legal, but they were certainly unethical. Burly assured the men that he would not hesitate to expose them if they did not give him the information he wanted. They asked him why, and he refused to answer.

"Names!" he said. "Give me the names; that's all I want, and you will never hear from me again."

What happened next surprised even Burly. Horowitz and Cline left the room while Herald stayed behind with Burly. Burly wished he had a gun or something for protection. Herald was a big, muscular black man, and Burly wasn't sure what Herald's instructions were. Within moments, two large men resembling bodyguards for high-profile criminals entered the room.

"Remove your clothing," Hearld commanded. When Burly started to protest, Hearld looked him straight in the eyes, nodded toward the two men, and said, "Do you want them to remove them for you?"

Burly's mouth went dry, and his palms grew moist. His heart pumped so loudly he could hear it beating, and he was sure everyone in the room could hear it, too. He had agreed to meet them there because it was a public restaurant, even if they were in a private dining room. If they wanted to hurt him, they wouldn't do it here. Would they?

"We need to know if you're carrying or if you're wired," Herald said.

Burly stripped down to his shorts and handed each piece to Hearld without protest, who passed them to the men. They patted down his clothing and carefully passed a magnet over them. "The shorts. Drop 'em." ordered the biggest of the two men.

Burly hesitated before following the request, but he didn't physically protest. "Drop 'em and turn around," the big man repeated. Stock was going to pay a lot for this, Burly thought as he lowered his shorts and turned his backside toward the two men.

"Bend over." Another command,

After this humiliating search, Burly quickly put on his clothes. The men in dark suits exited the room silently.

Mr. May, I have been instructed to give you two pieces of information and no more. The first is the name of the couple you are requesting. The second is a warning. Should the information I am about to tell you ever be traced back to our firm, you and you alone will be held solely responsible, Herald said methodically. Burly wondered how many others had been held 'responsible' and where they were now?

It wasn't the words that frightened Burly; it was the manner in which they were delivered. Burly believed his life was in danger. "Do you understand, Mr. May?"

"Yes," Burly answered quickly, "yes, I understand."

"Jonah Clyde and Harriet McMillen. You have received your warming already."

The suite of offices assigned to Levi Horowitz of Horowitz and Cline was locked. The only sound coming from their office space was the consistent whir of a high-powered paper shredder.

Burly couldn't believe his good luck. He had solved both cases. Victoria McMillen was the daughter of CJ Williams, and more importantly, she was the attorney in a lawsuit defending against her brothers and sisters. Stock was going to shit.

Chapter 34
Kate and the Siblings

Questioning of the Ohio Gas Company officials did not go well for Stock and his clients. Document after document showed that the company followed proper procedures. Every chance was given to CJ Williams to resolve the issue before his service was terminated. His death resulted from negligence or carelessness on his part and poor housekeeping. The Gas Company could not be held responsible for its customers' actions.

Victoria was constantly on her feet, objecting to every attempt to assign blame to the company. Stock was starting to believe he was no match for this Yale-trained lawyer. Not only was Victoria outpacing him in court, but something was happening with his clients. It wasn't what they said; it was what they weren't saying that unsettled Stock. They didn't confide in him, claiming it had nothing to do with the case, but he sensed something was wrong. It didn't surprise Stock that the elder brothers were against Jesse, but what stood out was Mirembee's apparent support for them. Something was going on, and if they wanted him to win this case, they better fill him in.

Kate and Carmen arrived the next day, bringing media attention. Stock needed a break. A case that had started off so well had somehow turned sour. With Kate here, maybe he could persuade his clients to settle. They still had a much stronger case against Consolidated anyway.

"Mirembee, it's Kate. When can we meet?"

"Please, Kate. Call me Rembee. Is Carmen with you?" Mirembee responded.

"Of course. She knows everything. She's anxious to meet you and her brothers. Rembee, I have some information that might be helpful."

"What, what kind of information?" Mirembee asked.

"Not over the phone. Can we meet? Before court starts tomorrow?" Kate replied.

"Yes. Do you want our attorney to come?"

"No, just us. How about your place?"

Mirembee hesitated, "Kate, I don't think Carmen should see... "

"Listen, Mirem, uh, Rembee," Kate interrupted, "we've been there and done that. See you at . . . 7:00 A.M."

Kate hung up, and Mirembee wondered if she should have told Kate about Jesse. Jesse wanted to move after his confrontation with his brothers and sister, but Mirembee wouldn't let him. She told him that she understood and that she knew he loved CJ. As a result, he was more beholden to her than ever. Eli, remembering the year he spent with CJ, empathized with Jesse. Frank told him he should be grateful because CJ did not abandon him. Frank said he was the one who should harbor hatred toward all of them. But he didn't. All he sought was the money he believed he deserved, and Jesse had no business complicating matters.

It was Frank's idea to continue Jesse's tips to the other side, but this time, they would tell him what to say. And he was not to use Rembee's phone anymore.

Kate and Carmen arrived early. Mirembee was ready, but the others hadn't arrived yet. Carmen was gracious. She hugged and kissed her sister as if they were old friends. Jesse received the same warm welcome when he stepped out of the bedroom, and the same for the other brothers who arrived later. They were all captivated by this young girl. They had seen her on television, knowing she was their sister but not fully understanding the idea. Now, this lively child entered their world and touched something deep inside them. Like a magnet, Carmen drew them in. It was as if they sensed the bond between them and her. There was so much of CJ in her. Dreams that weren't suppressed but nurtured. Visions with potential but not yet fulfilled. Carmen was their future, unbound by the chains of the past.

"Have you found Jill yet?" Kate's question brought everyone back to the reason why they were gathered in the first place.

"No, and I don't know if we will." Mirembee's voice was discouraging.

"I have some information that might help. You can decide what to show the attorney," Kate said while removing a manila folder from her briefcase.

"What is it?" Frank asked.

"Letters. CJ wrote when," Kate hesitated "when he wanted us to get married and he gave them to me for Carmen."

"CJ wanted to get married?" Jesse asked.

"The old man still had it!" Eli chuckled.

Ignoring the brothers' comments, Kate continued, "I was to give them to Carmen when she was old enough when I told her about her 'real' father. He wanted her to know about each of you." Kate noticed Frank's face. "He suspected you were his child, Frank. You are in these letters."

"Jill! Did he write about Jill?" Mirembee asked anxiously.

"Yes, but no information to help find her," Kate said.

"Let me see," Frank said, reaching for the envelope in Kate's hand. More than anybody else, Frank wanted to read what his father said about him.

"We'll have to wait, the court starts at 9:00," Mirembee said, ending the discussion.

Chapter 35

The Split

The crowd around the courthouse wasn't a full-blown media circus; a sideshow was a better way to describe it. Major outlets like UP and AP were noticeably missing, but Star, The National Enquirer, and Jet Magazine sent reporters and photographers. Carmen waved, smiled, and said her lines just as Kate coached her on the plane. "I want to be with my brothers and sisters," Carmen said into the cameras.

Victoria requested an immediate recess right after the court session was called to order. Judge Linton granted the defendants a twenty-four-hour break based on her request. While Victoria didn't reveal the exact reason for her request, she told the judge that it was of great importance and personal nature. Fifteen minutes later, Victoria met with Stock to discuss a settlement offer for the Williams siblings.

In a small private office at the courthouse, Stock told his clients he had received an offer. The $100,000 offer was meant for Mirembee, but the other supposed siblings had to agree not to sue the Gas Company either individually or together. We have twenty-four hours to decide on their offer.

"I don't need twenty-four hours. Tell them the answer is no." A defiant Mirembee exploded.

"Just a minute, Mirembee. This case is costing a lot of money. At least take the time to think about it." It was Stock's turn to explode. Softening, Stock said, "I could offer a counter of three hundred thousand. Maybe we could settle on two hundred."

"I won't change my mind!" Mirembee shouted.

"Will you guys talk to her? I think she's making a big mistake. You could all end up with nothing. At least, you could split the two hundred." Stock said, trying to hide his frustration, but the sweat on his forehead and the pulsating vein in his neck showed his true feelings.

"What do you mean split?" Frank asked.

"He means Rembee will get all the money, and we won't get a motherfucking dime," Eli said.

"Wait a minute," Jesse said. "Rembee already said 'No. Let's just give her and Stock a chance."

"They want to divide us. To separate us and make us fight each other," Mirembee said, looking at Kate and Carmen, who were silently witnessing the widening rift between Rembee and her brothers. Mirembee was certain that the white bitch of an attorney knew that her offer would cause this rift among the siblings. Just this morning, they felt connected, thanks to Carmen. Now this.

At Mirembee's apartment, they settled in to read the letters when the phone rang. "It's Stock, meet me in my office in thirty minutes. Burly got something. It's big. Bring everybody." He hung up without waiting for a reply.

Eli said. "They must have upped their offer to you." He left off the sister part, much to Mirembee's relief.

"Eli, I am not going to accept anything that leaves any of you out. Don't you know that by now?" Mirembee shouted. "You are my family. I will not let anyone or anything separate us again."

Stock and Burly were waiting when they entered Stock's office. Stock began, "You know Burly here has been working on finding your sister." Heads turned to Burly, who looked more like the schoolteacher he used to be than like the private detective he was now. "I assigned Burly to locate your missing sister. But then you asked me to get something on Victoria Headley, the gas company attorney. I gave that case to Burly, also. Well, he believes he has solved both problems. But I will let Burly tell you all about it."

Burly explained the process he used to investigate both cases. Systematically, he conducted a step-by-step review of the events, carefully omitting the names of the lawyers and the incident at the restaurant. When he finished, he simply stated, "It appears that Victoria McMillen is your long-lost sister."

I'll be goddamn! Eli offered. "She's white. Man, ain't no way that bitch is my sister. You must think we're all a bunch of fucking fools. This shit's gotta be your way of getting paid twice for the same damn job. You damn sure coulda come up with something better than this shit. I'll be fuckin' goddamn..."

At the end of Eli's nonstop tirade, Mirembee said, "But her eyes are blue."

"She wears contacts," Burly said matter-of-factly. "Here is her optical prescription." He handed the paper to Mirembee, but Frank managed to snatch it before her.

"What other proof you got?" Frank asked.

"I don't have proof. Evidence, yes. But no proof. I would need to talk to some of the principals involved to get proof," offered Burly.

"Who?" asked Kate. The siblings had accepted Kate as Carmen's spokesman and did not object to her questioning this man.

"The adoptive parents and Victoria herself. Before I do that, I wanted to know exactly what you want me to do." Burly was confident in his information, but he understood it would take time for his employers to absorb everything.

"We've found Jill?" Carmen's words were more of a question than a statement. It congealed the scattered thoughts in the room.

'Yes, baby, it means we've found our sister." Mirembee was on her feet, and Carmen quickly moved into Mirembee's arms. They held each other for a moment, and soon Jesse joined them. Eli and Frank looked at each other but remained seated.

"What does this mean?" Kate asked Stock, who was lavishing on the anticipated victory.

"It means we win the case." He said.

"There is something I still don't understand," Frank said. "My mom said that CJ had three girls pregnant at the same time. Elijah and I are six years apart, but according to Burly, Victoria is at least ten years younger than us, and you and Jesse are, I mean, it can't be you, Jesse or Carmen. I don't get it."

William's siblings had a hard time understanding the information from Burly.

Mirembee was beside herself with thoughts. Incomprehensible—that was what it was. Victoria was her sister. Their sister. Mirembee tried to recall her from the courtroom. Mostly, she remembered her dress. She wore designer suits in court... coordinated suits without matching blouses or shells underneath. The white pearls around her neck had to be from Tiffany's, Mirembee thought. They matched the pearls in her earrings, which she wore every day to court. She looked too white, unlike Jesse, whose skin was darker than his mixed heritage would suggest.

A closer look revealed that she resembled Jesse and inherited Frank's sharp nose and Carmen's wide, oval eyes. Most importantly, Victoria had her, no, their father's mind—she was quick and intelligent. She planned her moves around what mattered and let go of what didn't. Why hadn't she seen it before? But now it was clear—Victoria was her sister.

Sitting alone in her car, waiting for the light to change, Mirembee decided what she needed to do. Convincing her brothers wouldn't be easy.

Chapter 36
CJ's letters

Victoria welcomed the four-day break from court. Judge Linton had granted the recess on Friday. Naturally, the court remained closed on Saturday and Sunday, with Monday designated as a holiday. It gave her time to spend with Will and enjoy being pregnant again by the only man she had ever loved. Her case was going well. Even the partners had congratulated her on the brilliant stroke of genius that made the one child the sole heir. Her plan was working. She could tell by how the siblings entered the courtroom that a rift was forming, even though they continued to sit together in court.

Victoria expected the defense's strategy to include obtaining evidence to prove the paternity of the children. Neither she nor the partners expected Mirembee to accept the first offer. When she counters their offer, it will be rejected, and the siblings will be driven further apart. With luck, she could settle this case quickly with minimal monetary loss to her clients. It would be considered a victory.

Her thoughts briefly shifted to the bastard children of Clarence James Williams. She wept. Here was a poor, fallen man who fathered these children with six different women and cared enough to include them in his handwritten will. Her mother, her biological mother and father, had given her away without so much as a glance back. In a way, these illegitimate children were better off than she was. At least their father loved them.

Victoria loved the McMillens. They had given her more than she had ever dreamed or hoped for. Her mother loved her, and her father lovingly accepted her. She always felt that he wanted a son, his own son, but he got Victoria instead, and she suspected he remained slightly disappointed, although loving, to this day.

Victoria rubbed and patted her swollen belly. "I will always love you," she said to the child growing in her womb. "I will never give you away. No one will ever take you from me... no one."

Mirembee went back to the apartment and found her brothers, Carmen and Kate, sorting the letters.

"Rembee, this one is about you," Jesse said. Mirembee slowly dropped her coat on the chair closest to the door. Kate and Carmen sat on the sofa Mirembee bought from a thrift store. Frank and Eli were in the two matching occasional chairs given to her when Louise redecorated for the tenth time. They were the newest items in the apartment. Jesse was sprawled on the floor with the handwritten letters spread out in front of him. She positioned herself on the sofa next to Carmen, and Jesse handed her the letter.

"Read it out loud," Carmen said.

Dear Carmen,

I don't know how old you will be when you read this, but I wanted to tell you about your sister, Rembee. Her real name is Mirembee. You remind me of her. Both of you are smart and destined to succeed. The only difference is that your mother can see your potential, while Rembee is stifled by her mother. When Rembee makes an emotional break from her mother, she will become somebody. That is the Rembee I hope you will meet someday. If, when you meet her, she is still under her mother's control, she may not embrace you. Forgive her. With her mother, she has not truly embraced life.

She has suffered much at the hands of her mother. She may seem tough and indifferent, but that is not the real Rembee. That is her survival mechanism. She is not the woman she will become; that transformation will happen later. If you ever need anything, call Rembee.

She has built a wall of coldness around her, but she will soften when she finds love. Maybe that love will come from you. I tried to give her love, but her mother even stifled me. Finally, Carmen, my dear sweet Carmen, help Rembee see herself as I see her and as you will see her. The stars are her heaven, and if she only reaches high enough, she will capture them for herself.

CJ

'If she only reaches high enough, she will capture them for her own.' Mirembee let the words her father had written about her stay in her mind. She bowed her head and closed her eyes. I will, Daddy, I will capture the stars, I will, she mouthed.

With all eyes on her, Mirembee felt the silence. She turned to Carmen and said, "I love you, Carmen! And I love all of you," she said, waving her arm across the small room. You are all the love I need."

Holding back tears, Jesse said, "And we love you too, Rembee."

"I want to read Frank's letter next," Carmen said, smiling. "He's the oldest. Frank wasn't sure if he wanted to hear what his father had said about him, but he took the letter from Jesse and started to read.

To my dear daughter Carmen,

Your oldest brother is Frank. I want you to get to know him because I never had that opportunity. He was born when I was young, and I didn't even know he was my child until he was five, although I always suspected he was mine. His mother is very kind, and I know she has provided a good life for Frank and herself. When you meet him, please tell him I've tried to see him and to be his father. But his great-grandmother said I wasn't his father. Once, I tried to see him, and she got Harold Jr. after me. He beat me up pretty badly, and after that, I just let it go. I watched Frank from afar, and I am genuinely concerned about the man he is becoming. He's too much like his uncle Harold. He uses people and doesn't care how much it hurts. He needs you more than anyone. You can show him life's true value—the important things. Ask him to forgive me, and let him know his mother is special. The only way he can ever repay her is by being honest and doing for his children what she has done for him. Be careful, Carmen, Frank doesn't trust anyone, and he will be suspicious of even you. It's up to you to earn his trust and confidence.

CJ

If Frank hadn't been who he was, he would have openly rejoiced at this revelation from his father. If he hadn't inherited so much from Uncle Harold, Jr., he would have embraced his sister as his father wished. If his great-grandmother hadn't drilled into him that his father wasn't nothing, he might have seen the love his father had for him between the lines.

He uses people. Frank doesn't trust anyone—too much like his uncle Harold. Well, now we all see what he really thought of me," Frank spat out the words.

"I think you are missing the point, Frank," Mirembee said, feeling a new compassion for her brother.

"He loved you, but not how you treat others," Mirembee

said.

"What the hell do you know about it?" Frank's voice revealed the anger that was rising within him.

"Lay off, man. You ain't heard nothin' yet. Wait until we get to me. You'll look like an angel." Eli's statement reminded them of his presence and eased Frank's anger. "That is if he wrote anything about me."

"He did," said Kate. Jesse, please give Eli his letter. Carmen smiled knowingly.

"Eli, read it out loud!" Carmen yelled after watching his face contort.

Had anyone else in the room said that, Eli would have lashed out. But not at Carmen. He did exactly as Carmen commanded.

My Sweet Carmen,

You have three brothers. I had the privilege of naming only one of them, Elijah. I chose his name because I knew he was my legacy. Elijah is a genius. He does everything he can to hide his genius, but if you look deep within him, you'll see it. Don't be fooled by his manners and streetwise attitude; they are part of his effort to hide his true nature. He will be the hardest for you to love.

His mother, Lucy—well, Lucy had hard times, but Eli is devoted to her. There's much good in Eli, which he tries to deny. He took care of me when he lived with me that year. I got really sick, and Eli nursed me back to health. He prepared my food, washed me down with alcohol, and changed my soiled clothes when the food came out both ends. We couldn't afford a doctor back then, and Eli was my doctor. When I got better, he went back to his disguise, but he didn't fool me one bit. I knew it when he was born, and I know it now. He's just scared to let anyone see how smart and caring he is. When you talk to Eli, try to get him to live up to his potential.

CJ

"That's bullshit," Eli said. "He was a drunken old man. Not sick, just drunk. What the shit does, did he know. I ain't no fucking genius." His brothers and sisters listened to his words of protest while observing him with prolonged stares.

"If he's wrong about you, then he was wrong about the rest of us. I bet he didn't call me no genius." Jesse argued.

It was obvious that the brothers and sisters agreed with Jesse. Eli saw their agreement. Carmen moved across the room and sat on Jesse's lap.

"Here's your letter, brother Jesse." Carmen smiled, picked up one of the remaining three letters in the pile, and slid it into his hand.

Something about the way she said 'brother' caused Jesse to

regret what he did to betray his siblings. He did not mean to hurt this young innocent. It was just that Rembee had everything, and he was jealous. Yes, jealous. There it was. Out in the open, if only in his head.

"I'm sorry," Jesse said, nearly in tears. I know you all don't believe me, but I am sorry. I really didn't mean to hurt any of you. It's just that… well, Rembee… I just wanted what Rembee had, what CJ promised me. A home with a family." Jesse's eyes filled with tears. Kate, hoping to spare him more pain, took the letter from his hand and began reading.

Hello Carmen baby,

I've always wondered why the Lord blessed me with so many kids but so little money to care for them. I promised Jesse that one day I would have a house where he could live with me and Rembee. I love Jesse very much, even though he probably shouldn't have been born. I mean, he wasn't expected or anything. You might say he was a surprise, nearly as big a surprise as you were. Amy, his mother, never thought highly of herself and never discouraged Jesse from wanting anything. I taught him how to use his hands to make a living and to desire a family. That's what he needs now—a family. Jesse must never live alone. I made sure he knew Rembee, and maybe that was a mistake. He loves Rembee, and she will love him when they meet. The important thing about Jesse is that he must never live alone. He has lonely thoughts, but his being is social. Let him stay a part of your life.

CJ

Kate finished reading while Jesse leaned over to hug his little sister. Mirembee said, "Jesse, you will always have a home and a family with us."

"My turn. Carmen said excitedly.

Dearest Carmen,

You are the apple of my eye. God, give me life so I can give you life. When you were born, I was dead. My heart, my will, and my spirit were dead. Your mother, Kate, resurrected me and gave me a new life in the form of a beautiful baby girl. You are my flower bud to the world. The entire world watches you blossom into the beautiful orchid that you are. I owe you my life. You are forever loved. I feel blessed to have truly loved two women in my life, and your mother is one of them. My advice to you, sweet Carmen, is to never settle. When you marry, marry a man who loves you as much as I loved your mother. You will always find happiness if you do.

Your daddy, CJ

Not even Mirembee had received a 'your daddy' signature from CJ. Carmen was special. Carmen beamed with pride. Kate hugged her daughter, Rembee joined in, and even Frank, Eli, and

Jesse hugged their little sister. There was one letter left, and the siblings were anxious to read about the sister they did not know.

Blessed Carmen,

I wish I could tell you more about your other sister, but I can't. I hope and pray she has a good life somewhere. Her mother, Silky, was sent away to have our baby. Everyone said she got rid of it, but I know that's not true. Silky wouldn't do that. I saw her once after our child's birth, and she told me it was a girl, but that's all she would say. I know she moved somewhere on the West Coast, but I don't know exactly where. Please try to find her, and when you do, tell her that her pops would love to see her and look into her eyes to see what love has made.

CJ

They finished reading the letters. Each sat with a letter in hand, with Carmen and Mirembee holding each other's letters.

"We have to win. We have to win for CJ, our father," Mirembee said, sounding like the epilogue of an extremely long book.

"What about our other sister, the lawyer?" Frank's question pulled the group back to their current situation.

"I have a plan." Mirembee studied their reaction before revealing what she considered a despicable but necessary plot.

Chapter 37

The plan

Victoria was relieved after the three-day rest. Her pregnancy was progressing well, and she and Will spent their spare time building a nest. "Will, what do you think we should name her?"

"Willford Headley, the fourth. What else?"

"That's a funny name for a girl," Victoria said with a smile.

A little unnerved by how the second settlement offer was rejected, Victoria found new resolve to win the case. What did these bastard children want? A million dollars? For what? She reviewed the court case so far. The plaintiffs had scored on a few issues, but they still needed to prove paternity for everyone except Mirembee. Our side, the way Victoria convinced herself to think about all her defendants, was ready. She kept her best for the final week. Her strongest defense: attack Clarence Williams' character or lack of it.

She was prepared when the gas officials were summoned by the plaintiffs. She would be ready with character witnesses. Previous employment records, communications, his financial statements, and any legal involvements he had were reviewed. Files were organized, labeled, and stored alphabetically.

Victoria was ready, but a nagging feeling that she had

forgotten something haunted her. Sleep initially came anxiously, then she finally settled next to the man she loved. The sharp ring of the telephone jolted her into full wakefulness.

"Hello."

"It's time to pay, Miss Law and Order. Can you prove YOUR paternity?" The question hit Victoria like a lightning bolt. Her body stiffened; her mouth dried out. Her mind couldn't find a response.

"Is yo daddy black, Ms. Attorney?"

The caller hung up without waiting for a response. Pins pricked her nerves, but she managed to steady her trembling hand long enough to put the receiver in her nightstand drawer without disconnecting. The next call might wake her husband, and she would have to explain to him. Explain to him. Why didn't she listen to her mother? She was wrong not to tell him. But she loved him so much. And he loved her. Right? It won't matter. It can't matter. They were expecting a baby. And this time, nothing would go wrong. He did love her.

This case was the root of everything. She planned to get Ohio Gas to offer half a million. Surely, that's more money than these... bastards had ever seen. They would accept it, and then this whole mess would disappear. Her husband would never find out.

"What did she say?" Mirembee asked Jesse.

"Nothing. I hung up just like you said."

"Okay. We'll call again tomorrow. Get some sleep. Court starts at nine in the morning." She didn't need to tell Jesse twice to go to sleep. But for Mirembee, too many thoughts crowded her mind, and sleep was impossible. 'Daddy, am I doing the right thing? What if she really is our sister? I must know for sure.

Victoria awoke early, dressed, and left home driving the BMW. Thirty seconds after entering her office, she called Stock.

"I have another settlement offer." She informed him.

"Let's hear it."

"One half million, with the previous stipulations remaining."

"My. My. From one hundred thou to a half million. Methinks, I smell a turkey roasting." Victoria couldn't see his face, but she suspected Stock was smirking.

"Look, Richard. You know and I know that you have to discuss the offer with your clients."

"That I will. And I will certainly tell them what I think they should do with your offer."

It's a good deal, Richard. You should tell your clients to accept it. You know you'll get nowhere when we present our character witnesses. It's a final offer. Take it.

"I'll inform my clients." Stock emphasized the s, making sure Victoria understood that he represented all the siblings.

Victoria thought she could hear a chuckle in his voice as he hung up the phone without a goodbye.

She called Ohio Gas's legal department and informed them that it was time to reach a settlement.

After some discussion, she convinced the company attorney that she could negotiate a settlement not to exceed half a million. Victoria knew that liability insurance would cover up to two million and pushed for more, but he would not budge. She wanted to tell him it wasn't his fucking money, she was desperate, but not that desperate. Now, she had to convince Stock and his client or clients, or both.

Judge Linton was eager to grant a delay to allow the parties to discuss another proposed settlement. He would love to settle this. His docket was full, and civil cases rarely resulted in high-profile move-up-the-ladder results. This case was unusual but had drawn little publicity, most of which was about the young child star, Carmen. A settlement now would not be unwelcome.

"I say we take it," Stock told the siblings.

"Did she say if the offer goes to each one of us or just to Mirembee?" Frank asked.

"What she said doesn't matter. The offer goes to all of you. Divided six ways, it's still close to 100 thousand each." Stock explained.

"Minus your share. Right!" Eli offered.

"Tell her," Mirembee carefully chose her words, "tell her we will take one half million apiece, including our unnamed sister."

"I get it. If she accepts. She'll get part of the half million also." Jesse said.

"Mirembee, that's more than we're suing for. You can't be serious." Stock said.

"Tell her," Mirembee said defiantly.

Stock returned to the room after thirty minutes. "She wants to meet with Mirembee."

"No. All of us or no meeting." Mirembee said.

"Mirembee, meet with her," Kate said, looking over at Stock.

"Alone?" Mirembee asked. The siblings nodded.

"No!" She said.

Victoria did not sleep that night, waiting for the call she knew would come. She answered before the first ring finished. "Hello, Ms. Attorney. Got a message for you. Six A.M. Gateway

Inn coffee shop on Superior. Be there."

"No, no don't hang up. Wait." Her pleas went unanswered. The phone buzzed in her ears. She began to cry. The baby kicked, and she cried harder.

She arrived at the coffee shop at 5:30, only to find it was closed. The sign in the window read "Hours 6:00 to 12:00 midnight." She went back to her car and saw Jesse waiting for her. Victoria's heart raced. It was dark, and she couldn't see anyone else around.

"We knew you would be early," Jesse said.

"What do you want?" Victoria struggled to maintain control. "I know who you are. You're one of the Williams plaintiffs. What do you want?"

"We want to talk to you," Mirembee said in her most calming voice stepping from behind the car.

Victoria whizzed around to find Mirembee, Eli, and Frank staring at her. "I'll call the police!" She said desperately.

"And I'll call the newspapers." Responded Frank.

Somewhat gaining her composure, Victoria stated, "I can't talk to you without your attorney. Its. . . it's illegal. I could be disbarred."

"Why did you come then?" The question stumped Victoria momentarily. Why did she come? To save her family, that's why.

"Okay, let's talk. But not here. My office."

"No," said Mirembee, "My office." Jesse and Mirembee drove with Victoria the short distance to Mirembee's and Jesse's apartment, followed by Frank and Eli in Frank's car. When they arrived, Kate and Carmen were waiting for them.

Victoria remembered her small apartment in New Haven. During her senior year, her parents let her move off campus into a flat above a small sporting goods store. The furnishings were simple, but Victoria had painted and added yellow, blue, and pink flowered curtains over the windows. A couple of her artist friends gave her prints, which she matted and framed herself. Her parents insisted on a new carpet, which the landlord didn't object to because they were paying for it. Victoria chose yellow because it reminded her of the sun, and she felt New Haven needed more sunshine. The new carpet led to a new sofa and chair. Her parents also insisted she take the old bedroom set from home, with plans to buy a new one after graduation and moving back home. Her first apartment felt like a mansion compared to this place.

Its bleakness greeted her. The place looked scrubbed to the nth degree. No dust or dirt was visible, except for the white lampshade, which was faded yellow. Kate and Carmen sat on the pre-owned sofa. The two relatively new chairs, the only other seating options besides the straight-back chair, looked out of place.

From what Victoria could see, clean dishes were stacked on the drainboard, air drying. Nothing matched—no cup, saucer, or plate shared the same pattern, and the tableware was just as eclectic. This is the home of someone who turned down a half-million-dollar settlement, Victoria thought.

"You can sit here," Mirembee said, offering Victoria the straight back chair.

"Hello, Victoria," Carmen said, greeting her with a smile. She looked at the child, without altering her expression.

"If anything happens to me, all of you could be charged with kidnapping," declared Victoria.

Eli wanted to tell her to shut the fuck up, but they agreed to allow Mirembee to do the talking.

"Victoria, we have reason to believe you are," Mirembee hesitated, and Carmen blurted out, "our sister."

Victoria looked incredulously at the child, then at Mirembee, then at the brothers, and said, "You all must be crazy. I'm getting out of here." Victoria's attempt to stand up from the chair was blocked by Eli, who was quicker and standing over her.

Mirembee continued speaking, "You were adopted by the McMillen family when you were just an infant."

"That's no secret," Victoria said. "Everybody who knows

me knows that!" she announced. "If you think you can use that information to blackmail me to get what you want, you can forget it."

Mirembee ignored her protests and proceeded on, "Your real mother's name was Gillian."

"Stop! You have no right." Victoria was on her feet starring down Eli, daring him to try and stop her.

"Your father was Clarence James Williams." Mirembee was consistent in telling the story.

"You don't know what you are talking about. I am getting out of here." Victoria turned and started for the door.

"Before you leave, you better read this. There is documentation at the end." Frank thrusts the packet in her face. The cover reads INVESTIGATION OF VICTORIA MCMILLEN. She stopped and took the papers from Frank's hand.

"Please, Victoria, sit down," Mirembee said. Victoria returned to the straight-backed chair and opened the envelope. She read the papers quickly, a habit she'd developed from law school. Her mind could sift through a mountain of data, extracting only the important facts. All eyes were on Victoria as she read. She carefully absorbed the documentation included with the investigative report. Her pulse stopped when she read the name, Ann Silky Jillian. She wondered if the siblings noticed. She was trying desperately not to react. Another skipped heartbeat happened when she read about Clarence James Williams. The siblings noticed.

The reference to her blue contacts made her look up at the ten pairs of grey/green eyes staring at her. She then shifted her grey-green eyes, now hidden behind the blue contacts, back to the papers. The copies of the two birth certificates and the death certificate caught her off guard.

Her parents hadn't told her she was named after the child they lost. She knew her parents had a baby who died, but she did not know she was given the child's name. Despite all her efforts, she cried as she listened to the exchange between Ann Jillian and the investigator, which was clinically written by Burly. 'Let sleeping dogs lie.' was quoted by Burly in his report.

Victoria finished reading the papers. Carmen was the first to speak. "Our father wrote us letters. This one's for you."

Victoria looked at this girl and saw herself. For the first time, she noticed the resemblance. She read the letter.

After what felt like an extremely long silence, Victoria announced, "I'm pregnant. My husband doesn't know. He knows about the adoption, but he doesn't know about, about this," she said, waving the envelope in the air. "We don't want to hurt you," Mirembee said.

"Well, what do you want?" Victoria was crying.

"We want you to work for us," Mirembee said.

"Work for you? I am already compromised just by talking to you without your attorney. Tomorrow, I must resign from this case. What can I do for you?" Victoria was surrendering.

"Help us sue Consolidated Electronics. They stole our father's invention and made millions from it." Mirembee was insistent.

"So that's it. That's why you wouldn't settle. You could get more money from Consolidated." Victoria's quick mind was on overtime.

"Partly. Once we found out you were our sister. We couldn't settle. Since you would be getting part of the money, I knew somehow it, it wouldn't be legal or something." Mirembee said.

"What's the other part?" Victoria asked.

"We need money from the Gas Company. We owe for our father's funeral and, well, you know how much a major lawsuit like this costs." Mirembee knew Victoria knew. "Yes," Victoria said, "I know."

"Will you do it?" Mirembee asked.

"I have to talk to my husband first," Victoria said, drained. "I will call you. You won't need to wake me up in the middle of the night anymore." Her eyes caught Jesse, who lowered his head.

Regaining her legs, she steadied herself against the stained end table. "I will withdraw from this case today, but not before I talk to my husband. Tell Stock not to oppose my motion for a delay."

"Okay," Mirembee said.

"Victoria," Carmen smiled, "we love you."

Victoria gave the child a long, hard look and then embraced her.

Chapter 38

Victoria and Will

Judge Linton, appearing annoyed by the numerous delays, granted the motion to recess since the plaintiffs did not oppose it. The siblings marveled at how composed Victoria looked, given her state of mind forty-five minutes earlier. "She is very good," Mirembee whispered to Eli.

"Damn good!" Eli said out loud, causing the Judge to raise his gavel before lowering it without hitting the mantle.

"I just hope she's good enough," Frank said.

Victoria mentally rehearsed her conversation with Will a hundred times before she called him at the prosecutor's office. "I have something to tell you."

"Is the baby alright?

"Yes, of course."

"Are you alright?"

"Yes. I just want you to come home early."

"I'll be there at five ten. I love you darling."

If he truly loved her, her parentage wouldn't, shouldn't matter. Victoria waited until Will took off his coat and changed clothes before asking him to come into the kitchen. It was her favorite part of the house. Everything was blue and white. She had prepared a dinner of steamed clams, roasted vegetables, a three-bean salad served with white wine, and Boston Cream Pie—the kind that she and Will, Jr. developed a taste for while attending Yale. It was the best she had ever made. Victoria wanted the dinner to be extra special since this might be their last dinner together.

The table was decorated with matching blue and white plates. Crystal Waterford candlesticks crowned the table. Flames from the white candles flickered in time with the breeze from the ceiling fan. She poured wine into the crystal wine goblets, a wedding gift from Will's mother. They ate while engaging in small talk, and then Will said, "Well, do we go to bed now and consummate this lovely occasion, or do we wash the dishes?" This was what she loved about Will—his sense of humor, or was it his sense of timing? "Will," she thought, with no better way to say it but to just say it.

"Will, you know I'm adopted." Victoria began.

"Yes, you're one of the chosen ones," Will said.

She really loved this man. "There's more, I believe I know who my biological parents were, uh, are."

"Really, that's wonderful." noticing the look on her face, he added, "Isn't it?"

"My mother lives in Seattle. My father WAS ……. Clarence

James Williams."

Victoria waited for the reaction, which did not surface.

"Clarence James Williams, isn't he the one involved in that case you're working on?" Now Will was giving her his full attention as his mind tried to figure out what his wife was telling him.

"Yes. Only he's dead, and it's his children who are suing."

"But I thought they were all black. How can he be your father…?" The look on Victoria's face answered his question. His eyes shifted from her eyes to her stomach and back to her eyes.

Victoria was crying. "I should have told you, Will. I was wrong. I'm so sorry. I didn't mean to deceive you. Can you ever forgive me?"

Will Headley, II had always been his father's son. He hadn't taken a step in thirty years without first consulting his father. Now, the woman his father had approved for him to marry because she had the right pedigree stood before him, flawed. He was sure his father would tell him to cut her loose—do it now, quickly, and don't let it get messy. People might forgive a divorce, especially if the wife deceived her husband as Victoria had done. Get out now! His father screamed in his head.

"Vic, I will never forgive you… if you stop loving me. I will never forgive you if you do not let me be a part of our child's life. I will never forgive you if you die first and I'm left alone to rock in an old chair UNTIL my broken heart stops beating. I will never..." her lips silenced his voice. They held each other for a long time, and in his arms, Victoria decided to help her brothers and sisters.

The dishes remained untouched in the kitchen and Will smiled and rubbed Victoria stomach as they lay naked in bed. Victoria had never felt so completely a loved woman.

"Will, what about your parents?" Victoria asked, still unable to sleep.

"They'll claim I am adopted, and that's what accounts for my lack of Headley brains and charm."

"Will, be serious," Victoria laughed despite herself.

"I don't know," Will said sincerely, "I suspect this won't be easy. If he reacts as I expect, we'd better move to China."

"I'd live anywhere with you, Will."

"I'll talk to them tomorrow." Will got up and reached under the bed for his shoes. He felt the hard suitcase and pulled it out from under the bed. "What's this?" he said, opening the case.

"It is plan B.," said Victoria.

"Vic, don't ever leave me. Don't ever even think about it. I couldn't live without you."

Will, the first, was as predictable as a spring shower in April. Will watched his father rant and rave. He even allowed him to say nigger three times before he told him not to refer to his wife or his child by that label again.

Will, Sr. could not understand what had come over his son. The son, who had always folded under pressure from his father, was fighting back. When he told him to leave the nigger bitch, Will said if he continued to use those names to refer to his wife, he would never speak to him again. Will, Sr. had never heard his son speak with such determination, but that did not stop him from referring to his son's wife as a nigger.

Before he could think about it, Will, Jr. let fly a hard right his father's mouth. The blow drew blood and came as such a surprise that Will, Sr. dropped to one knee. The blow came as a response when Will, Sr. asked if he wanted to raise a nigger for a son. Will, Jr. was posed over his father, ready to hit him again when his mother stepped in.

"Stop it. Stop it! Right now!" she yelled from the depth of her voice.

"You don't know what he's done." Will, Sr. retaliated. "He is married to a nig…"

"He is our youngest son, Will, and the only one who is married and if you want grandchildren, then you had better accept your son, his wife and his child." Her mellow tone was the voice of reason, and Will, Sr. knew it, but pride goes before a fall.

"He's YOUR son." Will, Sr. said as he looked from his wife to his son and left the room.

"He'll come around son. Give him time, it's just such a shock." Will's mother said, hoping to mend the fracture.

"I love her, mother, and it doesn't matter to me if he does or does not come around. I'm going home."

Victoria was ready for the partners' meeting. The hardest part was behind her. Will truly loved her, and that was all that mattered. She would manage the partners.

"I am resigning from this case and the firm effective immediately." Mouths dropped, and eyebrows rose.

"You can't resign in the middle of a case. And you signed a contract with us for five years. There are three years left, and I'm sure you're aware of the consequences of breaking this contract, Victoria," the senior partner said.

"Do you need time off for the baby?"

"No, a conflict of interest prevents me from continuing with this case. You see, gentlemen, the plaintiffs have hired me."

"You can't do that. You'll be brought up before the bar." The senior partner rose to his feet.

"Victoria, have you lost your mind? Judicial ethics prevents you from accepting those plaintiffs as clients. You know that."

"Judicial ethics prevent me from defending a case in which I am related to the plaintiffs."

"What are you talking about? Explain yourself."

"Gentlemen, I will always be grateful for the opportunities you have given me. But. I have information which I believe to be true." "I…I am the daughter of Clarence James Williams."

Victoria's words were digested slowly, bite by bite. Their combined legal minds were forced into deductive reasoning.

Victoria was resigning.

Victoria was related to the plaintiffs.

Victoria was Williams' daughter.

Williams was black.

Victoria is black.

Only one other Black attorney, Harris, had worked at the firm, a fact that initially made Victoria hesitate. Her determination overcame her dissatisfaction, and she soon became immersed in the legal and social culture of the office. Her comfort level rose to the point where she believed she had formed friendships among the associates and earned respect from the partners. That belief was shattered by the next comment from the senior partner.

"Of course, we will relieve you of your contract under these circumstances, Victoria." Not even a 'We're sorry to see you go' Or a 'Thank you for the twelve-hours days you have given us for the past two years.'

"I thought so." Victoria's voice revealed the distaste she felt for the partners' lack of compassion or understanding.

"Oh, one more thing, I believe my sisters and brothers are willing to settle for the latest offer." She emphasized sisters and brothers.

"That ridiculous," Three partners said in unison.

"It wasn't yesterday." Victoria retorted.

"Victoria, it is illegal for you to divulge the insurance amount to the plaintiff."

I know the law, and I have not broken it. I don't plan to break it now by sharing any more information. I will no longer be involved in any matters related to this case. Scott has worked closely with me. He and Harry can continue to pursue it if that is your wish. My office will be cleared by 5:00 this evening. I will have an official resignation letter on your desk first thing tomorrow. Victoria's eyes scanned the room. I truly mean it—thank you all for the opportunity to work here. I have learned so much. You would be wise to offer others, like **me**, the same opportunity. Victoria left the room, but not before hearing the senior partner say, "Settle."

"Victoria, it's Rembee." "We agreed to settle the case for two million dollars. Can you believe it?"

"Yes, Mirembee, I believe I can."

"We are going to celebrate at my place. Can you come over."

"No, I want all of you to come over here. I want you to meet my husband. Seven o'clock. Okay? I'll tell you how to get here."

"We know." Mirembee said.

Chapter 39

The Siblings

Clarence James Williams' children sat at the large cherry dining table in Victoria's formal dining room. A tour of their home preceded the light pasta dinner and Caesar salad Victoria had prepared. Jesse was flabbergasted by the grandeur of it all. Eli mentally estimated the value of the original artwork visible throughout the lower level. Carmen did a tap dance on the marble floor and asked when they would open the pool, which was visible through the paned windows of the Florida room. Mirembee watched Will and quickly concluded that her sister had lucked out and that this man truly loved and admired his wife. Frank remembered his own upbringing and wondered what his mother would think of all this wealth. He smiled when he saw the sky-blue carpet in the study, recalling his great-grandmother's spit cup. His mother had scrubbed her carpet, but Victoria would probably replace hers.

The half-siblings settled in the great room for coffee, dessert, and dialogue. Mirembee began the discussion.

I promised Stock half of any award from the gas company.

"What?" Victoria was aghast. "He's entitled to one-third. One-half of two million dollars is a million. That's usury. He can't charge that a. It's . . . its unprofessional, unethical."

"We promised him ," Mirembee was quickly interrupted by Frank. No, you promised him. Victoria is correct. We don't have to give him that much money." Frank said.

"She promised for all of us. We better honor it. I don't like Stock. It's best we separate from him." Eli added this thoughtful comment.

"My agent gets twenty percent." The siblings turned to their little sister and laughed. Carmen looked disappointed, and Mirembee sensed her hurt at the laughter.

"Do you think Stock should get twenty percent, Carmen?"

"I don't know. But that's what my agent gets." Taking the cue from Mirembee, the siblings engaged in a genuine discussion about Carmen's statement. Carmen smiled, pleased with the insight her words added. She lay down on the white sofa and soon fell asleep. It was clear that Carmen was the glue holding the siblings together. Her innocence and unwavering love for each of them were obvious. Each of them reciprocated her love in their own way.

Stock should receive one million dollars—that's what he was promised—and he intended to hold them to their word. They also promised that he would be the one to sue Consolidated. Now that they've found their high-and-mighty white sister, they were planning to dump him. Thinking to himself, he mused, Stock doesn't take anything lying down. I wonder what the papers would think about the wife of an up-and-coming politico who was the bastard child of a black factory worker. As soon as he cashed that check, they'd find out.

Victoria's adoptive parents were extremely supportive of her decision to quit the firm and take up the case of her half-brothers and sisters. Money was not a problem and financial support was pledged by them for as long as necessary. Will's father remained livid. One phone call to his source ended with Will, Sr. screaming, "You fuckin asshole. How could you not know? Not only is the girl adopted, but she's black. You sonofbitch. My son is going to have a black child."

Will's mother secretly communicated with the couple out of fear of her husband and love for her son. His father's rejection brought mother and son closer together. Victoria worked alongside her husband, preparing the case against Consolidated Electronics. The lawsuit would be filed after their son was born.

"We are going to name him Clarence. After my father," Victoria told her siblings. It was a joyful occasion. They were all there—six children with grayish-green eyes and various skin tones, cooing at the contented infant lying in the cradle beside his mother's bed.

Carmen talked excitedly to the little baby. "You are my only nephew. And now I am an aunt. I'm so happy."

"He's not your only nephew," Frank said. The statement surprised the siblings, even though it shouldn't have, given their ages and their fatherly tendency to have children. "I have a son."

"Where is he? Can I meet him? How old is he? Does he live with you?" Carmen's questions poured out faster than anyone could answer. Mirembee held Carmen's hand and waited for Frank to respond.

Frank hung his head and answered all questions. "I don't know. But I intend to find out as soon as the trial is over. Then I'll have the money I need to take care of him."

"I think we should sue for the rights to the invention. We could manufacture the circuit adaptor ourselves. I know how to do it. CJ showed me." Jesse was excited.

The trial attracted media attention and centered on Victoria. The family connection between the lawyer and her clients became tabloid fodder. Mainstream media picked up the tabloid stories, and Hearst featured a photo of the siblings on the front pages of their five largest newspapers, with a larger inset of Victoria framed in white. Victoria negotiated the largest settlement ever granted in a civil suit for her siblings without going to trial.

Stock received his half of the gas company settlement, a cool million dollars, as promised by Mirembee. The sight, touch, and feel of the money made him settle. He would cash his check and wash his hands of these children. Just one more meeting with all of them, and he was done.

"We have enough money to manufacture the circuit adapter ourselves." Jesse said to his sisters and brothers amid the celebration of the Consolidated settlement.

"How are we going to do that?" asked Frank. "Do you know how to make an adapter?"

"I do," said Eli. "I know all about it."

"So do I," said Jesse. CJ taught me how.

"Well, I can handle all of the legal work." Offered Victoria.

"Frank, you can do the selling or marketing or whatever they call it. You are a good salesman," Mirembee said.

"What about me?" Carmen asked with all the sincerity of a child asking Santa for Christmas gifts.

"We will name the company after you, CAR-MEN Electrical, Inc. What do you think of that?" Victoria asked. "And Rembee, you can run the whole show as President and CEO." Mirembee smiled. Her sister had called her Rembee.

Money from the settlement with Ohio Gas was used to

pursue a case against Consolidated. Based on the outcome of the gas company's trial, Victoria had no problem convincing Consolidated to settle. "A million apiece for each sibling," Victoria offered at the first meeting. Consolidated agreed so quickly that Victoria felt she should have asked for two million apiece. However, the siblings decided that a million each, or six million dollars, was enough to build CAR-MEN Electrical. "One more thing," Victoria told the Consolidated lawyers, "you have to agree to stop manufacturing the CJ's adaptor and to buy the product exclusively from CAR-MEN Electrical."

Wilson Myers was permitted to resign after the board learned about his attempt to cover up the Williams v. East Ohio Gas case. The new CEO did not want to follow Myers' example, so he quickly agreed to the six-million-dollar settlement. Money wasn't an issue, but the exclusive contract with an unknown start-up company could be somewhat problematic.

"I guarantee that this deal will be cost-effective for your company. Believe me, a trial will end up costing you much more if you lose. And you will lose," Victoria admonished them.

Chapter 40

The Surprise

"Stock wants to meet with all of us one more time. I told him we would come to his office tomorrow. Let's meet here at 7:30 for breakfast and then drive over there together. Okay?" Mirembee asked her siblings.

"How much is this going to cost us?" Eli shouted out.

"He knows what the settlement was," Frank injected, "He will probably want half."

That night, Mirembee welcomed sleep as a welcome visitor. She had settled her debt with Louise, paying exactly what she owed and not a penny more. Although Louise was annoyed, she was fully aware of her daughter's newfound millionaire status. Mirembee felt content, satisfied that the ties binding her to Louise were finally severed. Tomorrow, she thought, anticipating the final meeting with Stock, I will be finally liberated from the past. I will live a future unfettered by past constraints. With that thought, she drifted to sleep with a smile on her face.

Stock studied the eyes of Ohio's newest millionaires. "Congratulations," Stock began. "It's great news about the Consolidated settlement." The siblings stayed silent, wondering what Stock wanted with them. "I know you are wondering why I asked you to meet this morning," Stock said as though reading their minds. "I have been contacted by someone who wants to meet you, all of you."

Stock escorted a strikingly beautiful woman into the room. She looked to be about the same age as Mirembee and Jesse, tall and poised. Victoria noticed she was wearing an **Oscar de la Renta** knit dress, carrying a Prada bag, and matching shoes. Her Dior sunglasses resembled those worn by Audrey Hepburn in Breakfast at Tiffany's. It's not money she needs, Victoria thought, glancing over at Kate.

She was one of those whose racial background wasn't immediately obvious. She had a light olive complexion and a face with firm features, lacking distinguishable Negroid lips and nose, but with very dark, curly hair that hinted at some African heritage.

Without removing her sunglasses, she let her eyes linger on each of the siblings a second longer than necessary before walking over to Mirembee and stopping. "You are Mirembee, correct? And you must be Frank since you appear to be the oldest," she said to Eli.

"No, my name's Elijah, this is Frank," pointing to his brother seated on the other side of the table.

"Yes," she said. "I should have known. "…and you are Victoria, the famous lawyer." She said, making eye contact with Victoria.

"And this beautiful young lady has to be Carmen, who…"

Before she could finish, Carmen blurted out, "Who are you? And how do you know all our names? Are you a lawyer, too?" The adults in the room kinda snickered before turning their attention back to the woman.

"No, Carmen, I am not a lawyer. My name is Simneetra. I am an author.

"Do you write books?"

"Yes"

"I want to be an author, but I already have a job. I guess I will have to wait until I retire," Carmen revealed.

"I hear you have a great job now."

All eyes in the room were fixed on the women talking to their little sister. Who is she? What does she want? Collectively, their minds came to the same conclusion: MONEY! She directed her gaze to the gray-green eyes of Victoria, Rembee Carmen, Frank, Elijah, and Jesse before speaking.

"You know what a Rolling Stone is?" Kate quickly covered

Carmen's mouth; Clarence James Williams was a Rolling Stone. That's why he fathered all of you... and me. I am your sister," she said, removing her glasses and revealing her gray-green eyes.

"Money," Eli said loud enough for all to hear.

"I don't want your money; I have my own. That's how I found you. What I want can't be bought. I want what you all have – what I never had – a family. Family is our father's gift to us. He didn't leave money; he left us each other. We have a chance to bond and become real brothers and sisters – a true family. All I want is to be part of your family. My next book is titled "Rolling Stone", and with your permission, I want to include each of you in it."

About the Author

Nadine McIlwain is a former Ohio public school educator who has earned numerous awards for excellence in the classroom, including the prestigious Milken Family Foundation National Educator Award. Locally, she was recognized for designing and leading the 100 in 100 campaign to restore the Greater Stark County Urban League, which was facing closure. Her leadership efforts raised $103,000, surpassing the goal of $100,000 in 100 days, and kept the agency open and active.

Her educational achievements, recognized at the local, state, and national levels, prompted the Canton City Board of Education to rename the district's administration building as the Canton City School District Nadine McIlwain Administrative Center in her honor.

"Rolling Stone" is her first novel.